Reaping the Harvest

By Robbie Cox

To Dan,
Thanks for being part of the magic!
Happy Reading,
Robbie Cox

First Edition

Cover art by SelfPubBookCovers.com/ktarrier
Cover graphics by Teri Edney

Editing by CTS Editing &
Weis Editing/Proofreading Services
Formatting by Sarah Mick

ISBN: 978-0-9905220-2-7
Library of Congress Control Number: 2014918705

Dedication

I would like to thank my editors-in-residence, the ladies to whom I owe a great debt and who forever keep me in The Way. To Charleen, Teri and Sarah, who are always pushing me to strive for bigger and better things and without whom my life would lose focus.

One

He fell against the coarse stucco of the church column, the rough texture ripping into his back as he oozed to the ground. Smoke floated through the morning air, carrying with it the scent of sulfur leftover from the burst of demonic power that had been used against him, red flames of energy that exploded from the demon's fingers. He suddenly wished he had kept his long coat on as pain screamed in his mind and explosions of white dots burst behind his eyes like Chinese fireworks. He barely managed to maintain his grip on the Guardian Sword. The blade pulsed a violent blue as warmth emanated from the bronze weapon. He could feel the power from the sword, but faintly, the voices of past Warriors a low murmur in his head instead of their consistent howl. His arm hung limp. Blood trickled down it and his chest from three long claw marks that left his flesh layered open revealing torn muscle and tissue beneath. His chest heaved with the deep pant of exertion. With gritted teeth against the pain, he attempted to control his breathing. And his anger. This should not be happening.

"What's the matter, Rhychard? Did my little scratch hurt?" The demon cackled, his voice like breaking glass. "Not as safe as you thought you were, eh?" The demon laughed some more, pleased with his ambush.

Rhychard Bartlett glared at the creature, the demon's arms waving in every direction as his eight-foot frame continued to prance around the parking lot. Vargas attempted to look human. He wore a black shirt, which covered his long arms and slender chest, and black pants that seemed like something from a fantasy novel. His talons couldn't be stuffed into his shoes any more than a bird's could and the curved nails of his claws scraped across the asphalt parking lot. His bluish-gray hair flowed about his head as he twirled, like sheers in a summer breeze. The demon's skin was a dusty gray and his blood-red eyes almost sparkled with the glee he was feeling, as his long clawed fingers twirled circles in the morning air. A happy demon. Oh, joy.

The Warrior of the Way held his sliced-up arm against his chest willing the blood flow to slow down. The pain was not as bad, however, as the knowledge of where he had been attacked. Vargas was *in* a church parking lot. How could that be? This was Rhychard's sanctuary, his safe place. He had been told that creatures of the Void weren't supposed to be on Sacred Ground. More lies. More contradictions.

"Surprised to see me, Rhychard? I knew you would be." Vargas stood on the white marked asphalt, hands on hips. "Imagine that, lied to by the supposed good guys. Ah, well, as long as their motives were good, right?"

Rhychard wanted to scream, not just because of the pain, but because he did feel like he had been lied to. This was not his war. He had been drafted and protested it with a simmering hatred. He wanted to kill Vargas. Hell, he wanted to kill the whole lot of them, good and bad, for screwing up his life.

He heard a little pop and a jingle of bells simultaneously and then Tryna's tiny hands were on his arm examining the wound. He felt warmth that eased his pain, but knew that was all she could do. Kree would have to do the rest. Still, it was enough for the moment. He relaxed a little as he felt the pain subside to a dull ache. "My little angel," he said with a deep breath. He tried to straighten himself against the column, but didn't have the strength.

"I am not an angel. I wish you would cease calling me that," she said in her childlike voice. Her burgundy dress flowed about her as if a breeze pulled at it, but the early morning air was still. "And if you make another crack about my size, I will tell Kree not to come."

Rhychard knew she meant it, too, and with the gashes across the right side of his body, he was in desperate need of Kree's help at the moment. Of course, Tryna was only half right. True, she was not an angel, but rather an ellyll of the Land Under, the realm of faeries. The part she was wrong about, however, was her size. Tryna stood two and a half feet tall, the top of her head not even reaching Rhychard's waist, who himself was five inches past six feet. The fact that she had the same proportions as a thin three-year-old, but the agility and skill of a seasoned veteran had been hard for Rhychard to come to terms with. She was also gifted with the magic of the faerie world, the ability to ease pain being part of it, for which at the moment he was quite glad. Tryna was an excellent nurse, even if her bedside manner left something to be desired. Still, Rhychard was never a good patient.

"Did you need help, Warrior?" Vargas taunted. "The ellyll is such a tiny little thing to help such a big, tough Warrior of the Way. I bet that mangy mutt will be along any minute now." The demon searched the vicinity, his gray neck turning this way and that.

As if he was summoned by the insult, Kree padded into view from behind the demon. The massive coshey, an elven hound of the Land Under, kept his onyx eyes on Vargas as he jogged to a spot between Rhychard and the demon. Then he just sat on his back haunches, waiting. Cosheys chose a Warrior to serve, becoming their conscience as well as healer and constant companion. Kree had chosen Rhychard and at first Rhychard wasn't sure what to do with the massive magical mutt. The furry elven canine had the body of a wolf, yet the size and mobility of a large lion. His back topped at just over four and a half feet off the ground with his head coming to just below Rhychard's shoulders. His paws were about the size of a bear's and his furry coat was glistening silver. When people had questioned Rhychard about him, the Warrior had just said he was a Newfoundland breed, raised to hunt bears. The coshey came in handy when solicitors came knocking on the door. One glance and people just backed away and left him alone, deciding that whatever they were pitching was suddenly not so important.

"And so he appears," Vargas said as he gave a mocking bow.

:You trespass, Vargas. You do not belong here.: Kree's mind speech was heard by the others. It was the communication of the cosheys. He could speak to several at once or to just one person of his choosing, faerie or human. He could also communicate from great distances to those with which he had a strong connection. When he had first spoken to Rhychard, it had almost put the Warrior into permanent shock. He didn't like someone in his head. His thoughts were his and he didn't like sharing them.

Vargas placed a withered finger to his temple and pretended to be deep in thought, his body bent almost in half and one leg stretched out in front of him, toes pointed outward. He resembled a court jester more than a demon. "And yet, I am here." He then pointed a long, clawed finger at the church. "And soon, my dear Warrior of the Way, I will be in there." The demon laughed as he vanished from sight, popping out as Tryna had popped in, the odor of sulfur in the air.

Kree sneezed. *:He makes my nose itch.:*

Rhychard closed his eyes and rested his head back on the column, the stucco digging into his scalp. "He makes my head ache."

Kree stood, turned in one fluid movement and then padded over to where Tryna sat with Rhychard. :*How fares the Warrior, Little One?:* Kree sent to the others.

"He needs you. Vargas was able to get too close," the ellyll answered.

"Hey, how come he gets to use the word 'little'?" Rhychard complained.

"He doesn't use it as an adjective." Tryna sat back on her heels as Kree moved closer. The elven hound pressed his massive forehead against Rhychard's shoulder. A tingling sensation coursed through him as he felt Kree's magic begin to knit muscle and tissue back together. He glanced down as his injuries seemed to shrink back in time, the open wounds finally becoming thin, pinkish lines of new flesh with blood the only evidence that something had happened. The pain was still a dull ache, but he was no longer in danger.

Tryna looked into Rhychard's eyes once Kree finished. "I knew you would be here, at this church, when I felt your pain." There was no accusation in her voice, only sadness. "This is not good, Warrior. This distraction almost killed you."

Rhychard didn't answer. There wasn't really anything to say. He came here to remember; he came here, to this church, every day for the past three months because it was as close as he could get to the love he had lost, the love he had lost because of being at the right place at the wrong time. Vargas had been doing his homework, apparently. He knew where Rhychard was going to be and attacked. Did he know why Rhychard kept coming here? If Vargas knew that Rhychard had a personal interest at Harvest Fellowship, it could put Renny in danger.

But Renny won't even talk to me now. Could he blame her? He knew that from where she stood it must have seemed like he went off the short pier right into the deep end. He was always vanishing to fight some sinister creature or investigate some bizarre disturbance. Yet, he wasn't allowed to tell Renny, not even to hint about it. It was against the Way of the Warrior as he had been told. Furthermore, it could put her in danger; make her a target to be used against him. Warriors did not have emotional attachments. *That's probably why they're all elves.* In the end it was more than she could take and she walked out. *In a dramatic flair, of course,* Rhychard smiled. *My Renny never did anything small.* He still had a scar over his left eye where the wine glass had shattered too close for safety.

Rhychard glanced down at the Guardian Sword in his numb hand. Its blade had returned to cold bronze. The broadsword, his inheritance from a dying elf, had an intricate design of vines engraved around the edges. Its pommel was encased with faeries cross, a stone resembling the bark of an ancient pine. It was supposed to help him draw upon the elemental magic around him, protecting him against the Void and its denizens. It held the memories and skills of a dozen previous Warriors who had wielded it before him. He wondered if they knew the number thirteen was bad luck. Whenever he pulled it out in battle, he could hear their voices and cries for action. Rhychard hadn't quite learned how to use that aspect, yet.

He laid the sword of power on the concrete beside him and tried to flex his fingers. Life was slowly returning to his extremities thanks to Kree's healing magic. It was one of the advantages of having an elven watch dog.

He hadn't asked for the blade or to be a Warrior. He had been happy in his life as a moving man, helping people haul their overabundance of possessions from one place to another. Simple. He liked the way his life had been before he even knew that faeries existed outside of Disney movies. He was about to enter his fourth year of the greatest relationship that had ever happened to him. He was even going to propose! Then he had to blow it and come across a dying elf. Jamairlo, Warrior of the Way, had fought the demons of the Void for one hundred and fifty years, Rhychard had been told by Tryna. Why couldn't he have waited one more night before getting himself slaughtered? Then Rhychard wouldn't be losing blood at the church where he was supposed to be getting married. *I should have stayed in my damn moving truck.*

Kree shook his head as he sneezed the sulfur out of his system, shattering Rhychard's thoughts of self-pity. *:How came Vargas to be in the parking lot, I wonder?:* Kree mind-spoke.

"Damn good question," Rhychard snarled. "Didn't you tell me this couldn't happen?" This was going to really suck if his last sanctuary was gone. Places of faith, whatever the faith, were usually off limits to the creatures of the Void. It was one of the many things Tryna had been sent to teach him when the Seelie discovered that they had a human as a Warrior. The battle of good and evil had a name, the Way and the Void, and it had nothing at all to do with religion. *If that ever got out a lot of preachers would actually have to work for their bread instead of jabbering their jaws.* However, wherever a gathering of people met that lived in the path of the Way that land became Sacred Ground and anathema to creatures of the Void. So steeped in the Way were they that creatures of the Void usually burned upon contact. That usually included the homes of righteous people, cemeteries of the righteous or even businesses that ultimately served the

Way. He had been told demons weren't supposed to be able to come as close as Vargas had.

"Something is not right here," Tryna said, her soft voice a child's soprano. "Sacred Ground is a haven. Vargas should not have been able to cross the sidewalk."

Rhychard gripped his upper arm where Vargas had ripped his flesh open. "Well, he was here, and faster than the sword could announce." This was not how he saw his life going. He wanted nothing to do with demons or elves or swords. He banged his head once against the cream colored column. He missed his old life. "Why didn't the sword warn me?"

Tryna glanced at Kree, but the elven hound just sat, his tongue lolling in the morning air as the day began to warm.

"Whispering about someone is rude," Rhychard said.

The ellyll nodded. "You are right. Our apologies, Warrior." Tryna stood with her hands behind her back. The wind pulled at her blond hair. She looked like a six-year-old giving a lecture to a room of dolls. "It's as I was telling you about your distraction with Renny Saunders. Your bitterness is creating a wall between you and the power of the Guardian Sword. Emotions can affect magic, for good or ill."

Rhychard closed his eyes. Another lesson. Another lecture. The past three months had been that way. "If your precious Guardian doesn't like my emotions, he or she or it can take this damn sword back. I didn't ask for it. I don't want it."

:It doesn't work that way, Warrior, and this you well know.: Kree mind-spoke.

He did know it. He learned the hard way that the Guardian Sword and he were bonded for the duration of his life. Rhychard opened his eyes and stared at the pale clouds above. "This isn't my life."

Tryna gazed down at him, her eyes almost sad. "Life is what we make on our journey through this existence. This may not be the journey you wanted, but it is the journey you must take."

Rhychard didn't say anything. He just sat there in a morass of self-pity mourning the life that had been stolen from him.

Two

Rhychard splashed cold water over his whisker-stubble face, the chill shocking some life back into his mind. His arm and chest throbbed with pain even though Kree had successfully healed the gouges Vargas had left. The skin was still pink and even the elven hound couldn't take away the scars that would be left behind.

He glanced up into the bathroom mirror, water dripping from his face into the dirty sink below. A hollow sunkenness seemed to surround his pine bark colored eyes. His high cheeks had a thinness to them that he hadn't noticed before. He knew he hadn't been eating properly, but didn't realize it had taken such a toll on him in so short an amount of time. He reached around and pulled his long dark hair into a ponytail, tying it with a leather thong. He noticed how his biceps bulged and his chest rippled as he did, more than they had before. While he had never been buff, he had had a few extra pounds on him, which he always blamed on Renny's cooking. The scars were pink and very visible in his dark curly arm hair. He was not the same man he was just a few months ago. He didn't look the same. He didn't act the same. He didn't even think the same. He had changed through no intention of his own.

He grabbed the towel that had been sitting on the bathroom counter and patted his face dry. With his hands pressing the terry cloth fabric to his face, he took a deep breath trying to steel himself. Three months ago life had been different. He had had a girlfriend. His business had been growing. Hell, even his sink had been clean. It wasn't even the same sink!

Now, everything was different. Now, he was a Warrior of the Way; the first human Warrior, at that.

"But you still need to eat, Warrior," he said to his reflection. While he was doing an elf's job protecting the world from evil, he still had a human's appetite, as well as very human bills. Being a Warrior didn't come with health benefits, a Christmas bonus, or even a paycheck.

He slipped a black tee-shirt over his head and left the bathroom. Kree lifted his giant muzzle from the arms of the couch as Rhychard entered the living room portion of his apartment, sneezing as the Warrior passed through.

:You smell funny.:

“Thanks. Not sure how to take that from a three hundred pound dog.” Rhychard lifted his shirt and took a sniff. “Okay, perhaps I do need to do laundry.”

:A shower might help, as well.: Kree laid his head back down, closing his eyes.

Rhychard just stared at the coshey a moment and decided to just end the hygiene debate where it was. “I’ll be back. I have a human job to do. You know, the one that brings in money so that I can buy those frozen pizzas you like.”

:Good, because the cupboard is quite bare. Do not forget the Guardian Sword. Vargas seems to appreciate surprising you.:

Rhychard felt the scar on his arm at the memory. Walking back into his room he grabbed his harness that held the Guardian Sword as well as two short swords made of iron. The faerie world hated iron, it seemed. It turned them to ash. He slipped it onto his back and as soon as the clasp was snapped the magic that was on them made them vanish from sight. He could still feel their presence on his back, but it was as if they had disappeared all together. It was one of the helpful tricks Kendalais, the Sidhe Warrior Master that trained him, had given Rhychard before tossing him to the wolves, or in this case the Unseelie. It allowed him to carry his weapons with him without being arrested. The minute he needed the powerful sword, he could just reach back, grab the hilt and draw it. It would slip into visibility and then the fight would be on. He still wasn’t used to carrying invisible swords with him everywhere he went, especially in an age where everyone used guns, but Kree had been correct. Ever since Rhychard was forced into the battle between the Way and the Void, he had become a target for the denizens of the Nether.

Once he was sufficiently armed against surprise attacks, he escaped the confines of his small condo. All Kree had said as he departed was for Rhychard to watch his back. “Isn’t that what the sword is for?” He had quipped back. Then he reminded himself that it hadn’t done such a great job last time.

My Hand Truck & I was Rhychard’s moving truck company. Most jobs he was able to do on his own, which worked out great for his wallet, but occasionally he needed help. Today was one of those days, so he swung by and picked up Trace Wheeler, who had actually landed the job for Rhychard. It was only fair to include him, although Rhychard could have used all the money himself. Kree hadn't been joking when he said the cupboards were bare.

Trace Wheeler was an old friend from high school who liked the idea of only working when absolutely necessary. That wasn't much as it stood, because Trace had never left his parents' home, choosing to stay with his mother after his father died of liver disease. Still, it worked out great for Rhychard because business had dropped off drastically since the Guardian had claimed ownership of his life. It was like being drafted into the Army. Your life was over and a new one begun. Furthermore, Trace never asked a lot of questions and was always available when Rhychard needed him, two things he required in a partner.

His friend only lived a couple of subdivisions away, so picking him up was never a problem. Within a few minutes of Rhychard leaving Whispering Oaks, Trace's portly five-eleven frame was riding shot gun and the two men were heading to the warehouse district by the interstate to empty out a storage unit for old Mrs. Ivey. Trace was also always ready to go because he never dressed up. He never really dressed down, either. His appearance was as shaggy as his walnut hair, which hung to his shoulders. He always needed a shave, but never had a beard. It was as if his whiskers grew so far and then gave up. He hid his small tortoise-green eyes behind sunglasses, whether the sun was out or not, which always made Rhychard wonder just how bloodshot they really were.

The job was simple. Empty the storage unit and dump its contents in the garage of her son, Justin. Trace came across the job because he was friends with Justin Ivey. "Well, not really friends," Trace had said in a lazy voice. "I just know him. He's pretty much a douche bag. A friend of mine told me they think Justin just wants to rummage around his mom's possessions to see what he can sell off before his siblings got their hands in the mix." Greed has no family loyalty.

Still, it was no business of Rhychard's. His job was merely to move the stuff. He was surprised, however, that Trace had even agreed to take the job if Justin's motives were that criminal. Trace had a soft heart, always rooting for the underdog. Rhychard had been that way once. Never again.

The windows on the truck were down and the heat of the August afternoon came through in the breeze, which wasn't much, bringing with it the tang of the nearby Indian River. Trace had been bellyaching about his mother since he plopped into the truck, as always, but Rhychard tuned him out, his mind still on Vargas's attack that morning. Besides, it was hard to feel sorry for a thirty-two-year-old that still lived at home.

Justin Ivey wasn't what Rhychard had been expecting. He assumed the man would have a small dirty tee-shirt over a beer gut, a four-day old beard and khaki shorts with the pockets hanging past the hems. In Rhychard's mind only white trash would steal from their mother. Instead, he was dressed in a suit with spit polished dress shoes. His blond hair was short and perfect and Ray Bans that probably equaled Rhychard's rent covered his eyes. He stood pole straight in front of an open storage unit, hands in pockets, feet slightly apart. He did not appear to be the douche bag Trace painted him out to be, but Rhychard had learned over the past three months that looks were often deceiving.

Since Trace knew the guy, Rhychard held back and allowed him to do all of the talking, which included getting their four hundred dollars. The Warrior leaned against the grill of his truck, arms crossed over his chest, and waited. Justin never took his hands out of his pockets, not even to hand over the money.

"Mom will meet you at the house. She'll have your money," he promised. "It's her stuff we're moving, so she's paying. Just stack it so I can move around."

Trace nodded. "Anything you need us to move inside? I'm sure your mom would love having her things back around her again." He shot Rhychard a glance as if he was supposed to be picking up on clues the other was giving. Rhychard just stared back.

"No. Just put it inside the garage and leave."

When creatures of the Void were around, the Guardian Sword would hold a blue glow to it and issue warmth that Rhychard could feel through the harness as well as his clothing. It was part of its protection magic that seemed to have failed recently. With humans, however, it was never that easy. They had learned well the art of deception and at times those who seemed good on the outside were decayed on the inside and vice versa. He had seen plenty of good people commit evil acts and people he could have sworn were demons in human form get all soft and mushy over a dying kitten. Creatures of the Void and the Way were black and white in their motives and actions, whereas humans were grayer.

Justin Ivey seemed shiny on the outside. However, what was inside the man? Rhychard saw the frown on Trace's boyish face. Why had his friend taken this job?

"Smart move, canceling the storage unit and saving the rent," Rhychard said. "I bet your mom's grateful for your sacrifice of space to help her out like that in these hard times."

Justin just glanced at Rhychard, both men hiding behind sunglasses. "What can I say? I'm nice like that. Now, how about getting started?"

Rhychard nodded. Justin was nice enough to sacrifice space, but not cash. "Sure thing boss."

Finally taking his hands out of his pockets, Justin stalked off. As if the warehouse district was going to stain his shininess. He was quickly behind the wheel of his Beemer and gone.

Trace ran his hand through his scraggly hair. "See what I mean? Douche bag."

Rhychard had to admit there was something off about the guy. He played the part of a man with money all the way to the attitude, but a rich man probably would have paid the storage fee as opposed to cluttering up his home. It was probable that Trace was right about the man's motives, but Rhychard doubted Ivy League Ivey volunteered his plans. Trace's friend could have just been making it up. People loved to create garbage about other people, especially if they were jealous of them.

It took about an hour to load the truck. The problem with monotonous manual labor is that while it keeps your body busy, it abandons the mind to venture into dark corners you wish to ignore. Rhychard's mind took him to what Tryna had said about the sword's power being hesitant because of his bitterness. The Guardian had drafted him into its war, given him a magical weapon to do battle with and then punished him because he wasn't all chuckling happy about fighting. Perhaps the races of the Seelie Court felt proud to be chosen as a Warrior, but Rhychard wanted nothing to do with it. Unfortunately, however, he couldn't get out of it. It was a cruel twist of logic that was thrust upon him and eventually it would cost him his life. Of course, without Renny, life had not been worth living.

By the time the last box was loaded, Rhychard's arm was throbbing and he just wanted the job to be over. Trace made a couple of cracks about Rhychard getting old and feeble and by the time the truck was loaded it was all he could do not to ram the Guardian Sword up the other man's ass. The only reason he held back was that he didn't want a lecture from Tryna on the proper use of his weapon or on Warrior behavior. It was worse than being scolded by his mother, which reminded him he should reach out and see how she was doing. She had taken his break up with Renny harder than he had.

"She's already family, Rhychard," his mother had practically screamed him into early hearing loss. "Four years you've been together. Four years! You don't just toss aside four years. We love Renny like a daughter. I don't know what you did to screw it up, but fix it!"

If only there was a way that he could. Yet, Kendalais had made him swear not to reveal his new mission in life to anyone. "Humans do not believe in the Seelie and they are safer for their ignorance." The human race was always seen as the weaker species, a fact the Sidhe Warrior Master took great pains to remind Rhychard. It would have made Renny and anyone else he cared about a target if they knew. As it was, the Seelie had put a protective detail around his family, something never before needed because there had never been a human Warrior before.

Kendalais was the elf the Sidhe sent to train Rhychard in the ways of the Warrior. He was an arrogant, pompous ass that had a sneer in every word he uttered. Rhychard, however, had made it perfectly clear that he wanted nothing to do with the elf, the Warriors, or their Guardian. He didn't care about the battle between the Way and the Void. He didn't care about demons or the Destroyer or how they wanted to destroy Rhychard's world. His world had already been destroyed. He just wanted to be left alone.

"I know we both need money and all," Trace said, his voice soft and distant as he stared out the passenger window. "But I don't feel right about this."

Rhychard stayed quiet, his hands squeezing the steering wheel.

"I mean, what if it was our mothers? My mom has a ton of stuff left over from before my dad died. It would kill her if any of it came up missing, you know."

After taking a deep breath, Rhychard asked, "What do you want us to do, Trace? We've already got the stuff. It's not like we can stand guard over it."

They rode in silence for a while, Trace lost in his sudden guilt and Rhychard sinking into his frustrations of life. As they neared the elaborate neighborhood of Sky Winds, Trace finally whispered, "It's just not right what he's doing to his own mother, is all."

"Why didn't you think about that before we took the damn job?" Rhychard snapped. "Life isn't fair, Trace. People are assholes. It's the way it is." He didn't need the conscience Trace was trying to stir up. Helping people got you screwed.

Rhychard backed into the driveway of Justin Ivey. As with all the homes in Sky Winds, the Ivey home was a neo-eclectic mansion that seemed more for show than living. It almost seemed like two homes with the garage positioned in the middle. The two sections were connected by more living space above the two and a half car garage, which Rhychard thought would make moving from one end of the house to the other quite annoying. Who would want to go up and then down a flight of stairs just to raid the kitchen during a commercial? The entire home was made of beige brick and while one half seemed like a Cape Cod home; the other gave the appearance of a Texas ranch. It seemed gaudy and pretentious. Rhychard's dislike for Justin Ivey increased.

The garage door was open and Mrs. Ivey stood to the side, dry washing her hands over one another. "Get out and make sure I don't run over any shrubs while backing up. Justin Ivey doesn't seem like a very forgiving man."

Trace stared at the elderly lady, her blue gray hair put up in a bun, her face a frown. "She looks scared."

"She's not scared. Now get out and guide me or you'll need to be scared."

Trace nodded his head as he opened the passenger door. Rhychard heard the man shout a greeting to Mrs. Ivey as he stepped out. Watching Trace's rotating hand in the side mirror, Rhychard caught a glimpse of Justin's mother standing beside him. She wore a peach dress with sunflowers on it and white tennis shoes. Her hands remained clasped together, the right constantly rubbing the left. Her eyes were a mixture of tears and a smile. Trace was right. She looked scared.

Rhychard took a deep breath. No. He was not getting involved. Interfering in other people's lives is what got him saddled with the giant glow stick strapped to his back as it was. He may be forced to battle the creatures of the Nether, but he was not foolish enough to keep poking his nose in the lives of people he knew nothing about. He had learned his lesson and the learning of it had cost him everything. They were there to do a job and they were going to do it.

It took them longer to unload the truck than to load it. Trace's heart wasn't in it and he just dragged along. He looked like a whipped dog the entire time; his whole body drooped as he tried to make conversation with Patricia Ivey while stacking her possessions in neat rows. She offered to make them lemonade and cucumber sandwiches, but Rhychard turned her down, just wanting to get out of there.

When they were finished, Rhychard sent Trace to collect the money. He just wished the lady a good day and slid back into the truck. He was hot and sweaty and wanted a shower and a cold beer. He hadn't expected the job to be easy, but he hadn't expected the emotional weight on top of it, either.

As Trace climbed into the cab of the truck, Rhychard glanced back through the side mirror and saw Miss Ivey caressing the edge of one of the boxes, her other hand covering her mouth. He could see the shake of her shoulders and knew she was crying. He tightened his grip on the steering wheel and pressed down on the accelerator.

Rhychard could feel Trace staring at him. "What?" He felt the seat shift as his friend leaned back against the passenger door, one arm along the back of the front seat, the other along the door. Trace was as drenched in sweat as Rhychard, his shirt pasted to his chest. Rhychard didn't look at him. He knew Trace was trying to make him feel guilty, but his friend was wasting his time. Rhychard felt guilty enough already.

"I don't get it," Trace said, his voice a tight edge. "You never would have just stood around like that. Miss Ivey is going to be ripped off by her own son and you just handed him her goods."

"What the hell? You got us that job, Trace. If you didn't feel up to it, why in the hell did you agree to take it in the first damn place?"

Trace turned his soft green eyes out the front window. In the reflection of the glass, Rhychard could see the struggle going on within. Finally, his friend said, "I thought you could help her. Protect her somehow."

"What made you think I could protect her? If she's being robbed, she needs to go to the police."

"The police won't help." Trace turned to Rhychard, his soft face tight with anger, "because nothing's been done to her...yet! By the time it happens, it will be too late. Besides, you helped that police captain. I thought you could help her."

"Well, you thought wrong." Rhychard's voice was more a sigh than a statement. "Helping Captain Relco was a fluke." *And it cost me Renny.* "I was at the wrong place at the right time."

John Relco had been the man Jamairlo had been protecting when Vargas and his gargoyles killed him. Rhychard had inherited the task of safeguarding him as he brought down the human half of the Unseelie crime ring, another thing of the faerie and human connection that made no sense. The Unseelie were helping a human crime lord sell drugs, so that they could prey upon the weak minds of the drug induced. Captain Relco was cracking down and Vargas was determined to kill him. Rhychard had saved the man, but not without the media finding out. He was named a Good Samaritan and had his picture in the paper. It hadn't been enough to save his relationship with Renny, but it did give Trace the idea that Rhychard was some sort of superhero. Miss Ivey wasn't the first hard luck case his friend had brought him.

A depressed Trace slid back around in his seat as he nodded. "I just felt bad for the old woman."

"So do I, but there's nothing we can do." It just didn't pay to be the good guy.

Rhychard pulled up in front of Trace's home and waited for his cut of the money and for his friend to get out of the truck. He had had enough of the guilt-ridden conversation.

Trace didn't move. "Well, we did what we could," he said in a sheepish voice as he stared out the window.

Rhychard fell back against the truck door. "You son of a bitch."

Trace turned back around, his face a mask of apology. "I'll get you your part of the money. I promise. I just couldn't take that lady's cash knowing what was about to happen." Trace opened the door and started to slide out. Before he had fully cleared the door he turned back, his face that of a scolded child who had just disappointed his father. "I'm sorry, Rhychard."

Rhychard said nothing as his friend shut the door. He just drove off.

The past three months had been an earthquake to his life. Nothing had been left standing. He lost Renny, his friends, even his ability to choose his own way, all because he stopped when he heard someone screaming for help. It was *only* three months ago, but it felt like yesterday.

Three

The air conditioning in the moving truck finally rebelled against the Florida weather and went on strike. Rhychard coaxed every chill blast out of it he could until only dry air coughed its way out of the vents. Even in May, Florida was too hot to go without at least a breeze so he was forced to ride with the windows down. The air was still sticky with humidity, but at least it circulated. He needed that breeze to help dry him off.

He had just finished a three-day move of office equipment for Brewster and Associates Law Firm from their old offices on Starks Avenue to their lush new paradise on Washington Street. It had definitely been a step up, too. They were now in a glass four story on the corner of Washington and Alamo taking up most of the block with the building and parking area. They had a great view of Downtown on one side and the Indian River on the other with plenty of fine dining and taverns nearby in order to schmooze the clients.

Rhychard was one of three private movers hired to assist in the transition. Now that it was finally over he was covered in sweat and grime, his long hair plastered to his forehead and neck while his black shirt was glued to his back. He was sore and tired and needed a shower.

Still, it was over and his night was truly about to begin. Rhychard slid his hand over the square box in his front pocket. Tonight he was going to take his four-year relationship with Renny Saunders to the next level. They had avoided this step for too long and he wanted to make Renny his wife. There was no reason not to. Saunders Realty was doing great. His moving truck company had a steady flow of business. Their lives were steady and calm. An engagement was just the thing to shake it up a bit.

Downtown was painted with night and bright balls of street lights. Revelers wobbled out of one bar and staggered down the sidewalk to their next open tab. A homeless man slept on one of the hard metal benches, his body wrapped in a raincoat as he used wadded newspaper as a pillow. The party crowd ignored him as they laughed dramatically at each other's jests. They were in their finest hitting-the-town attire, a stark contrast to the rags of the homeless man. They didn't even acknowledge that he was on the bench.

Rhychard pulled his truck to the curb. How people could just ignore someone in need, he would never understand. He opened the door to the back of his truck and pulled out two of the dark green industrial blankets he used to cover fragile items when moving them. He folded one into a tight square and gave it to the thin man as a pillow. The other he draped over the man like a blanket.

The man glanced up at him, his dark eyes reflecting his shocked acceptance as a smile pulled at his whiskered cheeks. "Thank you," he said with a voice of genuine appreciation and scratchy with years on the street.

"No worries, my friend," Rhychard said. "Sleep well." He closed the truck door and slid back behind the wheel. The people on the street were too busy with each other to even notice what had transpired. It was sad, really, but Rhychard knew it had always been like that.

As he slipped the gears into drive, a shadow flew over his windshield. Leaning forward he peered up, but whatever it was had flown out of sight. "Must have been a helluva bird." With his foot on the gas he headed into the night.

Whenever you're in a hurry, the Universe has a way of slowing you down. Rhychard took a deep breath, trying to calm his impatience as the railroad crossing bars sprang to life and cut him off from his evening's plans. Glancing in both directions, he tried to spot the light from the ill-timed train. Yet, there was no train in sight. No light. No blasting horn. No earth shaking rumble.

"Of all the times for a malfunction."

Another shadow passed overhead. As he glanced up, he could only stare. "What the…" A giant bat the size of a human being flew over his head. It was quickly followed by another. And then another. They were flying toward the back of a building lining the Downtown main drag.

Rhychard threw the truck into park and stumbled out, his eyes never leaving the sky. They were everywhere. He glanced around to see if anyone else had seen them, but the streets were quiet. Too quiet. Where had the partiers gone?

Reaching under the driver's seat, he pulled out the tire iron he kept there. He kept the heavy metal rod handy because even though most people didn't want to take on a six-five man, there were always idiots that allowed bravado to overtake common sense. He stepped in front of the truck, his fingers squeezing the solid iron in his hand. It didn't help him feel better. The skies were as deserted as the street. There was no sign of a coming train. Even the wind had gone into hiding.

Get into the truck, you idiot, and get out of here. He should have taken his own advice, but his feet were frozen into place. His heart beat a steady cadence in his ears. Something had him.

"Aiieeee!!" The scream pierced the night and chilled Rhychard's blood. Screeches of giant birds ricocheted off the surrounding buildings burying the second scream of agony.

He didn't think. He didn't even remember moving, but he was running for all he was worth toward the cacophony of shrill cries. It was almost as if whatever it was pulled him. He couldn't stop even if he wanted. He rounded the corner of one of those small twenty-five dollar a plate bistros, left downtown, and entered hell.

The giant bats he had seen flying overhead were attacking some man that appeared to be an actor for the downtown theater. The man had even brought one of the swords that seemed to match his Lord of the Rings attire. This, however, was not a show. The blond man knelt on one knee, trying to hold himself steady with a hand on the brick wall. His other hand held the sword that he was using to keep the creatures at bay.

Blood was splattered everywhere. The man's costume was tattered rags and his flesh was covered with bloody gashes. Whatever the creatures were they were determined to make hamburger meat out of their victim. Off to the side lay the remains of a wolf the size of a bear with a silver coat of fur drenched in its own blood. It was dead, chunks of its body ripped out and dripping from the yellow fangs of the beasts clutching the sides of buildings.

With the sword the man sliced at one of the talons of the leathery beasts. As he did another flew down and ripped at the man's unprotected head, claws raking across his right cheek and eye. His scream erupted Rhychard's frozen terror and spurred him into the fray. There was no time to think, only to act.

Holding the tire iron like a club, he swung at the creature that had sliced into the man's head, hitting its right shoulder and spinning it into the brick wall. Before he could think he stabbed the creature in the chest with the iron. The beast screamed and then exploded into a cloud of ash.

Rhychard just stared at the now empty spot, dumbfounded. The creature had just—poofed—into nothing. No body. No blood. Just...ash.

He heard a screech behind him and ducked as sharp claws grazed his shoulder. Pain blinded him as he fell against the wall. Turning, he saw the other man slice one of the creatures in half while still down on one knee before turning and running another one through. How he was even still alive, Rhychard had no idea.

Another piercing screech sounded above him and Rhychard thrust the point of the tire iron straight up trying to protect his head. A piercing cry shattered above just before ash rained down on him. Another of the dark gray creatures was flying in on the other man's blind spot. Rhychard hurled the tire iron like a javelin at the bat-like thing. It speared the creature's bulbous head and ash filled the air. The tire iron clanged to the pavement below.

The remaining two beasts flew away, shrieking their displeasure across the night sky. Rhychard rushed to the other man's side as he slumped to the ground, bloodied and battered. He had been ripped open in dozens of places and what wasn't gashed wide had been beaten black and blue. "Hold still. It'll be all right," Rhychard said, but he knew it wouldn't be. It couldn't be. There were too many holes in the man's body. Too much blood soaking his clothes and the cobblestones of the alley.

The man glanced up and the right side of his face was a mass of blood, one eye missing. It was all Rhychard could do to keep from vomiting. The man's lone eye was a deep ocean blue and shaped like a cat's eye, the pupil a narrow slit. He looked into Rhychard's face; his own a mask of confusion. "You're human?"

Rhychard nodded. Obviously the man was so far gone his brain had locked him into character. "Yeah, I'm human. Now, we have to get you to a hospital."

The man reached out and gripped Rhychard's wrist, his shaking hand still strong. "No, my friend. Your places of healing are not for the Seelie." The man coughed hard, blood spattering from his mouth. As the fit jerked him, his head fell forward, his hair shifted and the thin points of his ears were exposed. "The Guardian has called a human to take my place. These are changing times."

Rhychard stared at the bloody tips of the man's ears, not sure any longer that it was a man he was staring at. He fell back into a sitting position, gawking. Now he knew why the other had been surprised that he was a human. He had been expecting someone—something—else. "What are you?" He barely heard his own question.

The wounded creature had another coughing fit, blood pooling around his body, streaming down into the dirty alley. When he was done he said, "I am an elf of the Seelie, a Sidhe Warrior of the Way." He had to take a few deep breaths before continuing. "My name is Jamairlo."

"An elf? But," he took a deep breath, "But there aren't such things as elves."

"No time…to explain." Jamairlo held the sword he had been fighting with and handed it to Rhychard. The weapon glowed a deep blue and warmth could be felt in the bronze blade. "The gargoyles are coming back. You must protect the sword. You must save John Relco." The elf laid his head back against the brick wall. "It is now your destiny, Warrior. Wait for the Warrior Master. He will explain all."

"Wait a minute. I'm not a warrior. You have me confused with someone else." Rhychard shook the elf, but he was already dead. The sword grew warmer in his hand as a screech split the silence around him. Looking up he saw several of the leathery creatures darting through the trees, intent on the elf that was already gone. Rhychard gripped the sword as he sprinted for his truck. He had no foolish notion that they would not do to him what they had done to Jamairlo.

Rhychard jumped into the truck, dropped the sword on the seat beside him and jerked the vehicle into drive. The railroad guards were up. The night was silent except for the shrieks of the gargoyles as they dissected the body of the elf. The cab of the truck glowed a cold blue as the sword still warned of danger. Rhychard hit Washington Street and headed for home.

"Okay, this is not what I had planned for tonight." He could hear the quake in his voice and stopped talking. He had somehow stepped inside a fantasy novel and needed to change his boxers. Elves were real. Swords glowed. Gargoyles were more than a Disney cartoon. He kept squeezing and rubbing the steering wheel. This was a nightmare come alive and he would have thought it a dream except for the blood he was covered in.

Blood. Shit! Rhychard hit the brakes and slowed the truck down to normal speeds. He didn't need a speeding ticket now. There was no way he would be able to explain a sword dripping blood or the blood that smeared his clothes and hands. He needed to get to Renny, but not like he was. He would scare the hell out of her if he showed up like some horror movie. No, he needed a shower. Clean clothes. He should call the police. No. What would he tell them? Gargoyles attacked an elf? No, that was definitely out.

Think, Rhychard. Jamairlo said someone would come for the sword. Rhychard was just to wait. He didn't want to wait. He didn't want someone visiting him. He wanted to toss the sword into the river and be done with it. That's it. He'd throw the sword into the Indian River and rid himself of the whole business.

But what if they came for the sword and it wasn't there? The image of the elf's mutilated body flashed in his mind. That could happen to him. Or worse. No, nothing could be worse. Could it?

He tightened his grip on the steering wheel. *I'll keep the sword with me and go home. Then, once whoever comes for it shows up, they can take it and it'll be over.* What if whoever came for the sword blamed Rhychard for the elf's death? He hit the steering wheel with the palm of his hand as he let out a growl. Frustration pumped through his adrenaline-filled body along with indecision.

What are you going to do, Rhychard?

He wanted to call someone, but who was going to believe him? Renny would think he was nuts, Pastor Adrian would believe him possessed, and his parents would think he was drunk. There was no way he could get inside his apartment the way he looked. Someone was always poking their eye in a peephole searching for fresh gossip. They would see the sword and the blood and soon cops would be beating his door down. No, home was out.

The flower shop! He would go to his mom's flower shop and clean up. He kept some extra clothes there for emergencies whenever he helped her out. With the time of night it was, the place should be closed, so no one would see him.

Hopefully. It wasn't like the night had been normal so far.

Rhychard parked behind Blooming Petals and took several deep breaths. The crescent moon hung high in the silent sky. The air was still and sticky like the blood that clung to his memory. He locked the truck and held the sword downward, tight against his thigh. Within seconds he was off the street and inside. He thought of calling Renny. He should, he knew, but what would he tell her? He had lived it and he didn't even believe what had happened.

He found some rags in the back of the shop and wiped the now normal looking sword clean. Clean of blood. Clean of his fingerprints. He wasn't sure when the blue glow had disappeared. He had been too intent on the skies and the chance of those gargoyles finding him.

Once the sword was clean, he stripped down to his boxers and scrubbed hard at the blood that stained his skin. It had dried in the time it took him to get to the florist and was refusing to come completely off no matter how raw he scrubbed. He dropped his stained clothes into the can of cut stems and broken petals and tied it closed. He found the clean clothes and quickly dressed.

By the time he was put back together, his hands were a mere tremble compared to the shakes he had earlier. He stared at the sword on the plywood work table. What was he to do with it? Hell, what was he to do with anything that happened to him that night? He thought back to everything that had been said by Jamairlo. He was to guard the sword until someone came for it. Someone *would* come for it. He also said that the blade of the sword would warn him that those creatures were back. A quick glance showed that the sword was a normal cold metal.

He was safe for now.

At least, he was if the elf had been telling him the truth. For all Rhychard knew the elf wasn't really an elf and it had all been one elaborate prank at his expense. He could be on one of those hidden camera shows.

Except, no one jumped out and screamed, "Surprise! You're on Candid Camera." Rhychard swiped a hand over his face. Did all of this really happen?

He dug around in one of his mother's storage closets and found a small tarp she used to cover her flowers while in transit. He wrapped the sword and tied it with twine. He didn't need people seeing him carrying a sword around. He picked up the blue velvet box and stared at it. A tear filled his left eye, but refused to fall. This night was not going to go as he planned. He stuffed the ring into his pants pocket, tucked the wrapped sword under his arm and left out the back door.

Four

As the memory faded, Rhychard pulled into a far spot in the condo parking lot. Evening was coming on; the mighty oaks casting their long shadows over everything, and all Rhychard wanted was a shower, a beer and a cigar. The day had been a whole lot of nothing, and he was over it.

He knew that Trace was upset with him, but he couldn't help it. He was through sticking his nose where it didn't belong. He wanted his life back even though he knew that was never going to happen. Yet, while others may be guiding his destiny in some areas, he was determined not to make it worse in any other. His life was in enough turmoil.

Kree wasn't there when he walked through the door nor was Tryna, and for that Rhychard was glad. He had had enough people for one day. The silence was a soothing balm over his frazzled nerves.

He grabbed the last Amber Bock out of the fridge and peeled off his shirt on his way to the bathroom. Using his sweat-soaked top as protection for his hand, he twisted the cap off of his beer and took that first cold swallow. Pulling the bottle from his lips he took a deep breath and shoved all thoughts of Trace, Miss Ivey, and her lecherous son out of his mind. He stripped the rest of the way and stepped into the steaming water.

Of course, with everything else out of his mind, his thoughts went right back to where they always went—Renny. He had contemplated calling her again, but chickened out. Their last conversation hadn't exactly allowed room for friendly chatter. She actually accused him of being a borderline stalker.

The hot water beat the top of his head to waterfall down his face. *Face it, Rhychard, old boy, you practically were, chasing after her the way you did.* He had been pretty aggressive in his pursuit of reconciliation, he knew. Yet, four years they had been together. How could Renny have suddenly just switched everything off? He wasn't supposed to pester her anymore, so he had taken to visiting the small creek behind Harvest Fellowship. It had been one of their favorite places to just sit and be alone, staring at the calm water, soaking in the quietness and each other. Of course, he always made sure there were no activities going on at the church. He was pretty much persona non grata there since the breakup. The congregation had chosen sides and his wasn't the winning one.

Of course, that line of thought brought him back around to how Vargas was able to be on church property to begin with. It was one of the things that confused him as Tryna tried to teach him about the workings of the Way and the Void. From the little bit of reading and television he absorbed, it was vampires or witches or something like that that was incapable of entering a church. Tryna's only response was to ask him if he wanted to discuss fiction or real life. She had been teaching him for three months and he still wasn't sure of most of it.

It wasn't really her fault, though. She had never before had to teach a human the ways of faerie. She was used to an elf that already had a foundation of knowledge in The Way. The ellyll was the Keeper of Knowledge for the Warriors. Just as a coshey bonded to an elven Warrior, the ellyll bonded to an area, recording the history of a territory. Tryna had served Jamairlo the entire time he was a Warrior as well as the Sidhe Warrior before him. Yet, they weren't ignorant in the battle they fought as Rhychard was. They knew why they had been called and gladly accepted it. Rhychard knew nothing and even with Tryna's hard work the past three months, he still barely had a grasp on it.

What he was sure of, however, was that creatures of the Void, the Unseelie, couldn't enter holy ground. At least, they couldn't from what he had been told.

So how was Vargas able to attack him at Harvest Fellowship?

Rhychard took a swig of his beer as he left the bathroom, slipped into his room for some sweat pants and then headed for his porch. With a quick strike of a match, he took a long pull of his cigar and settled back into a worn out Florida State camp chair. The evening whispered a cool breeze through the branches of the oaks behind his condo. Dusk was beginning to blanket the town and his muscles screamed against the tension of the day. He was tired. Not just from the day he had, but from the life that was now his, the life he didn't want and never asked for.

He took a swig of his beer and stared out at the woods. He picked this unit because of its access to the miniature forest from his back porch. Kree had been drawing too much attention at his last apartment, which didn't allow pets to begin with. It was hard to tell his neighbors that the coshey wasn't his pet when this giant elven hound was always seen hanging around his place. Humans didn't understand a dog not being owned by someone. When he first said that Kree wasn't his, the property management people sent out animal control to try and catch him. Of course, how they were even planning on capturing an animal Kree's size was beyond his imagination as was what they would do with him once they had accomplished such a feat. Still, Rhychard decided it was best to move. Besides, that apartment had too many memories he needed to be gone.

He discovered the Whispering Oaks Condominiums while moving a senior couple out of one of the upstairs units. It was a quiet place surrounded by massive oaks whose branches intertwined overhead and shaded most of the back area. Shrubs and palm fronds cluttered the ground beneath the trees, but Rhychard had cut a path through to a small river that ran east-west behind the buildings. He found a flat rock that jutted out into the water that he could sit on and watch manatees relaxing in the cool water. The only people he had seen had been a couple paddling a kayak one time while he was out there. Otherwise, the river was pretty deserted, which made it all the more enjoyable for him.

His condo wasn't big, a small kitchen about the size of a walk-in closet with a dinette area next to it which opened into a small living room. To the west was the front door, to the south were sliding glass doors that led to his peaceful haven of a back porch and to the east the hallway to the smaller half of the condo, if that was even possible. Entering the hallway, straight in front was the tiny bathroom, to the right was Rhychard's room with a view of the massive oaks in back. Just to the left of the bathroom was the closet that held the washer and dryer and everything he wanted to hide from his mother when she would visit, which wasn't often because she was still mad at Rhychard for losing Renny. If you continued left you entered the guest room. It hadn't always been a guest room. When he first moved in, he decided to take a roommate to help offset the costs due to his new career as savior of the world disrupting his money making career. Brent Huckabee had been a college student partying on Mom and Dad's dime. At first, Rhychard thought it would work out. Brent rarely went to school, choosing to sleep all day and carouse all night. Since his parents were footing the bill for his college education and housing expenses, he really had nothing invested and treated it as a lengthy vacation.

At first, the different schedules made it seem as if Rhychard was living by himself, except for the piles of dirty dishes always left scattered throughout the house, that is. Clothes were also just tossed wherever the younger tenant stripped and the single bathroom resembled more of a locker room than a home bathroom. Varying schedules also meant someone was usually awake and while Rhychard tried to keep the noise level down for his passed out roommate, the other saw no need to return the courtesy.

Finally, Rhychard had enough and in the middle of the night evicted the college kid. His place wasn't big enough for obnoxious behavior. It was perfect for him, but he alone, and he had kept it that way ever since. Of course, Tryna had been right and he shouldn't have used the Guardian Sword to get the message across, but someone that inconsiderate had to be of the Void and in need of vanquishing, at least from his apartment. Now, if he could teach Kree to vacuum he'd be all set.

Rhychard took a pull from his cigar as he watched two squirrels digging in the ground for their horde of acorns. He was alone and he shouldn't be. Sure he had a three-hundred pound elven hound and a two-foot high faerie for company, but he didn't feel like cuddling up to either one of them. He should be with Renny. That was how it was supposed to be. He glanced over at the matching chair. Empty. He had set it up for Renny even though he knew she would never use it. It was a reminder of what he no longer had. No longer would have.

As he sipped his beer, he heard the familiar jingle of bells behind him. He didn't say anything.

"How is your arm?" Her voice was soft and almost as musical as her entrance.

He took a drag from his cigar. He knew he shouldn't be angry at Tryna, but she was the reminder of everything he had lost. She was the kitten he could kick when he couldn't kick those he was really angry at. After a moment, he answered, "It aches, and working today didn't help." He could hear the bitterness in his voice and it nauseated him. It was unfair, but he couldn't shake it. He took a deep breath. "I'm sorry. It's been a rough day."

Tryna walked over to him and placed her childlike hand on his arm. The evening breeze tugged at her red dress causing it to swirl around her tiny figure. Her blond hair fell past her shoulders to the middle of her back and her greenish eyes were pools you could swim in. "I'm sorry, too. I know the pain you feel is not really in your arm, but in your heart. I truly wish things could be different."

Rhychard gazed down at the small ellyll. He didn't trust his voice, so he just nodded.

Tryna squeezed his arm. "But Rhychard, bitterness is a plague upon the soul. To grieve what was is one thing; to live in that misery will only eat away at your being. The Guardian chose you because of the man you are. Do not allow your anger at that choosing to steal your goodness."

He glared at her. "Why not? Being the Good Samaritan cost me everything. The Guardian can call someone else if my bitterness disappoints him and I can have my life back."

She shook her head and it was like a five-year-old was showing him pity. "It doesn't work that way, Rhychard. The past is gone, but you can change the future. You are a Warrior of the Way. You are the protector of this world, your world."

He turned his gaze back to the swaying branches of the oaks. "The people I cared about in this world turned their backs on me. The rest can go to Hell or the Void for all I care." He glanced at his beer, downed the rest of it and set it on the concrete and his cigar in the wooden ashtray. "I'm going to bed. Good night." He pushed himself out of his chair and went back inside. He was through with this day.

Five

Rhychard massaged his bicep as he waited in line at Common Grounds for his first cup of coffee of the morning, black, extra caffeinated, and hot enough to scorch the top of his mouth on the first sip. He hadn't realized he had been out of his Eight O'clock Bean until he went to make some that morning and only then remembered he had used the last of it the morning prior. He hadn't been all that worried about it because he expected to have money that afternoon for important things, like food. Of course, that was before Trace had decided to be Mr. Benevolent without asking him first. It didn't really matter since he was out of anything resembling breakfast food, as well, and would have had to go out anyway. Luckily the coffee house around the corner from his apartment served bagels, as well.

His arm, though healed, was still tender from Vargas's razor sharp talons. Tryna insisted it was all in his head as Kree's powers had never failed, while Rhychard insisted it was all in his arm. Of course, he had never had can openers rip it open before, either. She had just rolled her eyes and popped out, which really wasn't a fair way to end a fight. However, that never stopped her from doing it when she could "no longer tolerate his human nonsense" as she put it. Sometimes she sounded quite a bit like his mother.

He took his cardboard cup of morning wake-me-up and found a quiet spot overlooking the busy street of Downtown. The street was a bluster of cars and pedestrians, each rushing to get where they needed to be before the clock struck eight. It had been a while since he had to worry about time as much. Becoming a Warrior had cost him not only his girl, but his moving truck business had slowed drastically due to his erratic scheduling conflicts. Trace was the one bringing in the most money, lately, he had to admit. Except for yesterday, of course. Evil has no sense of a daily job. Rhychard canceled too many appointments to make him a reliable business.

The Warrior popped the lid off his coffee to let it cool a bit as he watched a young yuppie walking his little Pomeranian. Not a man's dog by any sense of the word, but then again he lived with a canine the size of a horse. Of course, Kree would sniff his nose at being compared to a dog. *I am a coshey. Can dogs talk? No. They merely do pathetic tricks to please their owners and wag their tails. Most just lie around eating and defecating on the carpet.* Then he would ask if they were going to get pizza that night for dinner. Rhychard didn't care what Kree said, he was an overgrown watchdog sent to babysit the human Warrior.

Tryna had told him that the coshey had chosen to join Rhychard. Warriors always had an elven hound as their companion and they were bonded for life. When Jamairlo died, his coshey, Meelim, was killed with him. Rhychard hadn't seen the elven hound fight, but had seen its corpse. It had surprised the other Sidhe Warriors and the coshey when Kree left the Land Under and joined with Rhychard.

It was only one of several things that three months ago had changed drastically in his life and he had thrown the Land Under into a tizzy. There had never before been a human Warrior. Most humans didn't even know the faerie world existed nevertheless protected their own world. Rhychard wished he was still ignorant of it all, as well, but not only was he in the know, he was also in the battle, and so far it had cost him everything. The worst part of it all was that he couldn't tell anyone. He was alone in all of the insanity. The only two people he had to share his life with were an overgrown mutt and a midget that kept popping out on him.

Of course, that little midget has saved my life a few times. Yet, his life shouldn't need saving. He shouldn't have to walk around with a sword strapped to his back all the time. He should not be fighting demons or gargoyles or banshees or anything else that came out of an episode of *Supernatural*. He *should* be having dinner with Renny and planning their future.

He picked up his coffee and took a sip, the steam flushing his face. The hot liquid warmed his insides from the chill of his anger. Hindsight is a great teacher with painful lessons and even though he wished he never would have gotten out of his truck that night, he knew he wouldn't have done anything differently. When you hear a scream that freezes your heart you have to investigate.

It had been that characteristic that had made the Guardian choose Rhychard when Fate had sacrificed Jamairlo. There had been no other Sidhe in the vicinity and no time to wait for one. The Void could not be allowed to get a Guardian Sword, the magical weapon of the Warriors, and so to the bewilderment of the Sidhe, a human was chosen.

Rhychard took a bigger gulp of his coffee now that the temperature was at a drinkable level and watched as the yuppie's Pomeranian did number two on the lawn of a Mexican restaurant. *Now that's appetizing.* Once the miniature fur ball was finished, the owner dutifully bent over and retrieved the doggie doo with a plastic bag he pulled out of his pocket. *I'm glad I don't have to follow Kree around on clean up.* Then Rhychard laughed. *Of course, with the size of his piles of waste people probably think there's a bear in the neighborhood.*

"Rhychard? I thought that was you." Looking up Rhychard saw the balding head and plastic smile of Miles Evans, one of the few members of Harvest Fellowship he was glad not to have to tolerate anymore. That was one of the things about going to church Rhychard hated. You had to be nice to the idiots. "How have you been? I haven't seen you around the church in a while." Miles took the other chair at the table and helped himself to Rhychard's peace and quiet morning. He was an odd looking man with small ears; a nose that looked like it belonged on the yuppie's dog and very thin eyebrows. He was short and squat and his only exercise was pushing himself away from the table. By the size of him, he didn't exercise much.

"No, you haven't." Rhychard shrugged. Why is it church people only confront you about your attendance when they see you? They never go out of their way to reach out to you. Rhychard stopped going to Harvest Fellowship over two months ago and not one of the righteous had even called to hear his side of the story. "With Renny and I breaking up it was just too hard to go back. Besides, I've been extremely busy." He watched as the yuppie disappeared around a corner, bag of dog shit swinging in his hand. *I will never walk a dog.*

"I can understand that with Renny, but you really need to be in church. It's the right thing to do." Miles had a chocolate frappe in a plastic cup, which he sipped through a straw while beads of condensation left watery trails down the sides. *Fitting.* "Glad to hear you're busy though. I had heard your business wasn't doing well."

Rhychard was about to take another swig of coffee when he paused and glanced at Miles, his eyebrows raised. "Word gets around. I thought gossip was a sin." Actually, gossiping was the nation's real pastime; everyone just liked to say it was baseball. It had often been joked that religious people didn't gossip, they just shared "prayer requests."

Rhychard was sure he had been the subject of several prayer requests being passed throughout the church.

Miles waved a pudgy hand as if dismissing the notion. "Not gossiping, I assure you. It came as a prayer request at our last usher's meeting. Being Head Usher people tend to tell me things they want to pray about. We even prayed about it in the deacon's meeting."

"Of course." And probably the Sunday school meeting and choir practice and nursery workers meeting, as well. Rhychard drank some more of his coffee before he said anything he would just get scolded for later. Tryna would give him a long lecture on motive, which was the difference between the Way and the Void. He already knew how it would go. If people shared the story out of concern for him, then that was good. If, however, it was out of malice to ruin his name, then that was of the Void. The path you were living in life was really determined by the motives of your heart as opposed to actions. Some people just needed actions—rituals—to give substance to what was inside them, as well as to govern those actions and protect their hearts. Rhychard thought most of it was just semantics, but he was learning.

The Way and the Void weren't so much factions as they were entities. However, there were two camps and ultimately two leaders within the faerie world. The Guardian ruled the Way and the Seelie Court, which consisted of all the faerie races dwelling in the Land Under. The Destroyer was ruler of the Unseelie Court within the Nether and they were of the Void. Basically, as far as Rhychard could tell, it was good versus evil, but then again didn't everything in life boil down to that?

Miles continued to rattle on about the doings of Harvest Fellowship. Rhychard semi-paid attention as he watched the people walking past. He wanted to get up and leave, but he also knew he needed to discover what Vargas was doing at that church. While Miles was an obnoxious man of self-importance, he did have an inner ear to the happenings of what was going on at the church. He obviously heard quite a few prayer requests. If anyone knew the church's misdeeds, it would be the talkative Head Usher.

As Rhychard listened, he spotted a young Latina girl walking down the opposite side of the street. Her jean shorts were tight and short enough to reveal the cup of her ass and she wore a loose string top that readily advertised her lack of a bra as it draped over her ample tits. To make the ensemble complete she wore white heels Rhychard could hear clicking on the concrete from where he sat. Her long satin hair hung loose around her shoulders and swished across her back as she swayed her hips like a billboard advertising her wares. She was definitely for sale.

A gray sedan slowed as the driver passed her, then turned down the street in front of her and waited. Rhychard thought the car looked familiar, but couldn't place it. There were no distinguishable stickers or hanging gadgets from the rearview mirror. The girl didn't hesitate. She walked over to the passenger door and slid in. *She knows her date.* It could have been an innocent car ride, but in this part of town, dressed as she was, Rhychard highly doubted it.

"So, in two weeks we're beginning a Saturday night service," Miles said. "You should come and be my guest. Show those praying for you that their prayers have been working."

More like put Rhychard on display as the loser you turn into if you don't follow the rules. No, thanks. Of course, it would get him inside for a closer look. While he doubted there would be obvious signs of evil doings—church people were notorious for wearing masks—his eye might see something those not looking would miss. "I'll see what my calendar is like and let you know." Coffee empty, it was time to go. "Speaking of which, I have a job I have to get to now. It was good seeing you, Miles." *Okay, so it was a lie, but my motive was good. It kept me from hitting him.*

Six

Rhychard ran his hand through his long raven hair. He winced a little from the stiff pain in his arms, not from the previous day's attack, but rather from a full day of hauling filing cabinets across town. With Trace giving Miss Ivey back her money, Rhychard had to scramble to pick up work in order to silence his growling belly. He had called in a favor with Captain Relco and was hired on to help move old case files into storage. It wasn't a big job, but it allowed him to eat for a couple of more days.

The night was cool, with the scent of autumn in the breeze as it tugged at the colorful array of leaves just starting to turn toward fall. He stood outside the Harbor Townhomes and watched as Renny Saunders slid out of her Altima, the night air catching her long blond tresses in its invisible fingers, stroking it the way he used to do. He couldn't help but stare, remembering how that petite form had felt in his arms just a short while ago. She was wearing a soft teal business dress and carried her Giorgio Armani briefcase, bringing her work home. She probably wouldn't even look at it. She had worked hard to build her own real estate company and at one time she would have worked well into the night. That was a couple of years ago, however. Together, they had made a pact to keep the majority of their evenings free to spend with each other and for the most part, they had succeeded in keeping that commitment. Most evenings, they spent at home reading or watching some old movie. They had already been acting like a married couple for quite some time, which is why Rhychard had been ready to take it to the next level. Both their businesses had been doing well; they had the approval of both families. It was just logical to get married. Why would they keep waiting? Hadn't four years shown them enough of each other to make it work?

Of course, the night he was going to propose the Guardian decided to screw up his life. Rhychard slid a hand to his front jeans pocket where he still kept the engagement ring. He ran his fingers over the white gold band

and felt the bump in his pants that told him where the diamond rested. He never stopped carrying it. At first, he had hoped she would soften and change her mind. When it became obvious that Hell would sell snow cones first, he just kept carrying it as a reminder of what he lost.

Renny unlocked the lobby door to her town home and he watched as she started to climb the stairs. He wanted to go to her, take her into his thick arms and cradle her from the world's evils. He would protect her now as he protected her then, shielding her from anything that would stain her vision of a peaceful world. Just shy of thirty years, Renny was still innocent in all of the cruelties of life. She had been raised in the church and barricaded from what was really happening in the world for the most part. She didn't know about Vargas and the minions of the Void. No one did, but him. Rhychard wondered now if he should have told her. It was Kendalais who convinced him not to for fear that Renny would be made a target by those who would want to hurt Rhychard.

"There are reasons Warriors don't have families of their own," Kendalais said in one of his many tedious lessons. He was a Sidhe Warrior Master and it was he who had been sent to teach Rhychard of his new role in life, a role he did not want. "It is not merely for the safety of the family, but to protect the Warrior from being controlled by outside forces. No one must be permitted to know what you are or what you are doing. You must let the woman go."

Rhychard had not been given a choice. Not because Kendalais told him to stop pursuing her, but because Renny had made it restraining order clear that she wanted nothing more to do with him. She hadn't actually filed a restraining order as much as threatened it. He had lost her and there was no way of getting her back.

:This is no longer your path, Warrior,: Kree's deep voice sounded in Rhychard's mind.

The Warrior of the Way glanced up and saw the coshey perched among the thicker branches of the maple that Rhychard was standing under. He shouldn't have been surprised. "How you got up there I will never understand. Did Tryna send you to check up on me? Afraid I'd get blitz attacked again?"

Rhychard felt the mental equivalent of a shrug from the elven hound. *:It is what it is. We worry for you,-* Kree spoke. *-Why do you persist on chasing a path that has been closed from your journey? Being here will only cause you pain. This one chose not to be a part of your life anymore,* *even after your heartfelt attempts to persuade her. You cannot give what she is unwilling to receive.:*

"She deserved better."

Kree snorted in disgust. *:Well I remember the night she left. Why get slapped in your pride again?:*

Rhychard sighed. Why, indeed? "But how could she be expected to understand what I couldn't even tell her?"

The night that Renny left had been his fault. He had practically disappeared on her without any way of explaining where he went. His behavior had already been erratic since coming upon Jamairlo that night in a dark alley. The night he rescued Captain Relco, however, it all came to a head.

He had been hunting down Vargas because the demon was after the police captain, John Relco. The captain was close to uncovering one of the Unseelie's vast drug rings. Sad really that the supernatural would be dealing drugs, but these days everyone had their hands in it. The dark elves discovered that with the aid of drugs they could better control humans and use them to do most of their dirty work. Vargas had created a whole network of labs producing mind-altering concoctions in order to twist the minds of people. Captain Relco was just about to break it open when Vargas sent his army of gargoyles after him. Tryna caught wind of it just in time for Rhychard to intervene and save the man. However, saving Relco had cost him Renny.

Apparently, she had planned an elaborate dinner for him, soft jazz, merlot, a medium rare London broil with twice baked potatoes. He was supposed to have been there at seven, but gargoyles don't have watches and wouldn't stop the battle in time for Rhychard to call. Creatures of the Void would probably be a lot more understanding if they had wives to come home to. As it was Rhychard didn't arrive home until quarter past ten and when he opened the door he was greeted with a shattering glass of red wine followed by a plate full of bloody meat and cold potatoes. She was screaming and crying and the empty bottle of San Sebastian merlot told Rhychard she was very intoxicated, as well. She accused him of cheating on her, of not loving her, and of being the illegitimate son of homosexual llamas. He had kept that last one from his parents. Renny didn't storm out of his life as much as stumble, but the result was the same. She was gone.

Rhychard shifted against the tree he was leaning on as he stared up at the lighted window. Renny was still an active member of Harvest Fellowship. She had always known what was going on. Not like Miles, a busybody in everyone's business. She actually cared what happened to that church and the people in it. He doubted that had changed in three months. She should be able to give him a clue as to what was happening now, a hint, at least, of what Vargas was after on Sacred Ground. Surely, she would now be a great asset in the battle against evil. Yet, how would he ever be able to describe what was going on without her thinking he was certifiably crazy? He couldn't even get her to talk to him about normal things.

Rhychard wrapped himself tighter inside his full body leather coat, the one that made him appear as Hugh Jackman did in Van Helsing. He knew Kree was right. As much as they had promised each other to be a family, his new secrets were more than she could bear. Family sticks together no matter what. They work through their differences, supported each other. Tryna had warned him, had told him that she felt distance from Renny. He just hadn't wanted to believe it.

:Warrior, look.: Kree mind-spoke.

Rhychard followed his gaze to the top of Renny's building and felt an instant panic. Crawling along the roofline were a half dozen gargoyles, ugly creatures with hides like liquid leather, dark and damp. They were scrawny beasts with their skeletal structure visible under their flesh, and red, sunken eyes in hollow sockets. They had no hair or fur and bulbous heads that held long pointed ears. Their claws were like bird's feet with razor sharp talons and bat-like, sinewy wings that sprouted from the middle of their backs. Their mouths were a hideous mass of yellowish, jagged teeth that Rhychard had seen tear a man's arm off. These were not the Disney cartoon variety of evil. They were usually Vargas's vanguard. What they were doing at the town home, Rhychard had no idea. But he knew he wasn't going to allow them to remain. She might not want him to be a part of her life anymore, but he would be damned if he was going to turn a blind eye when she could be in danger.

Rhychard pulled the iron short swords from over his shoulders as he began to cross the street to where Renny lived.

:Warrior, you are borrowing trouble.:

"I'm fighting evil," Rhychard called over his shoulder. "Isn't that what your precious Guardian drafted me for?" He held both swords in his left hand as he reached inside his coat and pulled a knife from the brace he wore. He needed to get their attention off Renny's place and onto him. He flipped the point of the knife over, holding it between his fingers and waited until one of the creatures flew close enough to make it a target. As soon as one of the gray beasts did, Rhychard threw the knife, also made of iron. He tossed one of the swords into his right hand and then ran to the building. The knife plunged into the gargoyle's shoulder. The beast shrieked into the night and then disappeared. He loved the effect iron had on the Unseelie. He could do without the drifting ash, however. The other five shrieked their own warnings as they abandoned the building and dove after Rhychard. The Guardian Sword now blazed a blue heat against his back. He was not going to pull it and listen to the voices of dead Warriors, not when the iron swords would do.

Rhychard leaped onto a parked Nissan, jumping to its roof as two gargoyles dove at him. He braced, both swords held in front of him as he awaited the attack. The first came straight at him, its front claws reaching like groping hands, only these fingers ended in razor sharp talons. The other was zeroing in from the left. Rhychard sliced at the first, knocking the talons to the side with one sword as his second sliced across the creature's middle. The momentum of the gargoyle knocked Rhychard backward onto the hood covered in the ash of vanquished beast.

Without hesitation, Rhychard spun to his left, awaiting the second gargoyle's attack. The creature was almost on him when a grey blur dropped down on it with a roar that echoed off the brick buildings. Kree dug his fangs deep into the creature's neck and ripped the gargoyle's throat out. The coshey sneezed as the creature turned to ash.

:They taste as terrible as they look, I would have you to know. Not at all to my liking.:

Rhychard glanced up at the remaining three creatures as they hovered in the air staring at them, undecided as to what to do. "I thought I was borrowing trouble," He said. The closest gargoyle screamed at the human and coshey and then flew off into the night. The other two must have thought it was a wise decision because they quickly followed.

:We are bonded. Where you go, I go, even if it's into trouble.:

Rhychard glanced down at the silver elven hound. "Could they have been going after her in order to get to me?"

Kree turned his gaze upon the single light in the apartment above. *:It's possible, but why would the denizens of the Void have procrastinated such a move? They could have used her a few weeks ago when you were protecting the police captain and done themselves more good, rather than waiting until the present. Outside of the demon beginning to touch sacred ground, nothing is going on that we can surmise. What would be the advantage?:*

What indeed? Rhychard followed the coshey's gaze. Renny crossed in front of the window, turning the light off as she went.

Seven

He knew he should have been trying to discover why Vargas was able to step onto Harvest Fellowship property, but Rhychard couldn't get the vision of the gargoyles swarming around Renny's apartment out of his head. Why were they there? What did they want with her? Gargoyles were the hunting dogs of the Nether. They were used by demons and dark elves to sniff out their victims or as frontline soldiers, easily disposable. They were the grunts of the underworld, and he needed to discover why they were put on Renny's trail. Tryna would be pissed, but he didn't care. He promised to protect Renny and, even though she didn't want his help, he wasn't going to stand idly by and watch the Void destroy her life. At least, not if he could help it. And he could help it.

Rhychard revved his Suzuki GSXR1000 as he tried to balance a coffee and a mocha Frappuccino on his tank. Traffic was light, so he didn't have to worry about too much zigzagging through the Harbor City streets as he made his way to Saunders Realty. If Renny kept to the same pattern as she had for the last two years, she'd be walking out the door at 5:15 on the dot. While he wasn't holding out much hope that she'd agree to go to dinner with him, he was hoping the mocha frappe would at least halt her long enough for a couple of questions.

When Renny had first walked out on him, Rhychard tried everything to get her back. Nothing worked. She stopped answering his calls, ignored his emails and texts, and even threatened a restraining order if he showed up at her apartment again. She made it clear in no uncertain terms that she was through. Finally, Rhychard surrendered and left her alone. He hadn't talked to Renny in close to two months. Yet, he visited all the places they had frequented together just to be a part of her. That's how Vargas had found him at Harvest Fellowship. How he had been able to attack Rhychard was still the mystery.

He parked his bike next to her hunter green Altima, hopefully not appearing threatening at all. He wanted to seem harmless and inviting, but at six-five it was kind of hard. *I should have left my jacket at home.* After sliding out of the seat, he sat on it, holding both cups in his hands to help control his nervousness.

When she finally walked out the front door, Renny was too busy rummaging through her purse to notice him at first, but when she finally looked up and saw him, she stopped for a moment. He watched her take a deep breath to fortify herself before continuing to her car. *Always ready for a fight.* He had hoped two months would have softened her a bit. He was wrong, it seemed.

"What are you doing here?" Her voice was hard, poised for battle and full of accusations. She wore a dark gray business suit with a skirt instead of slacks and light gray pumps. Her blond hair was pulled back into a tight ponytail, which made her face look stretched too tight. She appeared harsh and it bothered him.

He didn't want to fight, couldn't if he was going to protect her. Before he answered, he held out the coffee house cup to her and tried to put on his most disarming smile. "Mocha Frappuccino with whipped cream and tiny shavings of chocolate on top." He held it out for her to take while he sipped his lukewarm coffee. Forty miles per hour on a bike will cool anything down. He thought he'd benefit if he took her on a ride to cool her exterior, but doubted she'd agree.

When she didn't take it at first he just shrugged. "It's just a drink. I'm not here to fight or beg you to come back or cause you any trouble." He shook the cup a little, drops of condensation falling to the asphalt below. "It's just a drink."

He could tell by the look on her face that she didn't believe him, but she reached out and took the drink anyway. "So, again I ask, why are you here?" She took a sip of the peace offering and Rhychard knew that was all the thanks he was going to get. At least she stayed.

"I ran into Miles at the Common Grounds and it made me wonder how you were doing." He cocked a smile at her as he tilted his head. "You said I couldn't come by the apartment. You didn't say anything about your work place."

She didn't return the smile. "Don't try to be cute." She sucked more of the melting brown liquid through the straw and then sighed. "You look good. Healthy. How've you been?"

He glanced down at his belly which was tighter than it had ever been. Fighting demons will do that to a person, he supposed. "I've been working out. I guess I have lost a little weight. I hadn't really noticed until now." He looked back up at her. "And how about you? Business holding up with this economy."

Rhychard listened to her go on about the housing market and having to let some agents go. He knew she hated that. Renny was loyal to the bone and would have sacrificed her own needs before releasing others. From there they moved on to their parents and how her mom wants to move back to Indiana and wants Renny to go with her. They talked about his parents, how his father just bought a sailboat.

"Someone told me you had a huge dog," she said, her Frappuccino almost gone.

Rhychard laughed. "More like he has me. He just showed up one day and never left." His coffee was cold, but he held the cup just to have something to do with his hands. "How are things at church? Miles said you guys were starting a Saturday night service for those too lazy to get up on Sunday morning."

She nodded. "Not this Saturday, but the following. You going?"

He spun the cup slowly in his hands. The conversation was lasting longer than he expected it to, but he still hadn't heard anything to explain why the gargoyles had been at her place or how Vargas could get onto Sacred Ground. "I was thinking about it. I miss some of the people there. Miles invited me to be his guest, but I'd rather sit with you if you'd let me. No meaning behind it. Just for comfort, you know."

Renny took a deep breath. "Rhychard, I'm seeing someone."

It was as if the Destroyer had wrapped his hand around Rhychard's heart and kept it from beating. He forced himself to keep breathing. It had been bound to happen. He should have expected it. Renny hadn't stayed single long between her last boyfriend and Rhychard. She loved being in a relationship. Still, hearing it hurt worse than Vargas ripping his arm open in three places.

"So, I suppose breakfast after church is out." He forced a smile. "I'm happy for you. Really. Who is the lucky guy?"

She shook her head. "It doesn't matter who he is. I just can't sit with you that Saturday."

Rhychard's brows pressed together toward the top of his nose as he gave her a curious look. "You can't tell me who you're dating?"

"I *won't* tell you who I'm dating. It's none of your business." She grabbed her keys tighter. "Look, I have to go."

"Wait, you're mad at me because I asked who you're seeing?" Rhychard stood and stepped to block her from her car door. Mistake. "That's not fair!"

Renny shoved him out of her way, which would have been funny to anyone watching since she only stood five and a half feet. "Not fair? Not fair! Not fair is you leaving me sitting alone all the damn time and never once telling me where you'd been. Not fair is you cheating on me! I'm not fair? I don't have to be fair to you." She jerked her car door open and practically lunged into her seat just to get away from him. She slammed the door as she started the engine. No goodbye. No screw you. Not a smile or even a middle finger. Renny just drove off leaving him standing there staring after her.

How could things have gone so wrong? They had actually been getting along quite well for a while. So what happened? How do you go from polite to pissed off in only two seconds? It made no sense.

Rhychard crushed his cardboard cup and tossed it to the ground, not that it made him feel much better. With his hands on his hips, he spun a couple of times in place as if the answers to his frustration would come by on one of the passing cars. Why did Renny have to be so infuriating? They were simple, casual questions for crying out loud! He stood staring at the cars whizzing by. A red Jeep slowed as it neared the stop sign. Rhychard stared at it a moment before it dawned on him that he knew the driver. David Morsetti. He was one of the main Sunday school teachers at Harvest Fellowship with about seventy-five in his class, which a couple of months ago seemed to keep growing and having to change classrooms.

Rhychard was about to call out to him when a slender girl slid out of the passenger side and started walking quickly away. David drove off, looking all around as he did for…witnesses? Rhychard looked closer at the woman and then realized that he recognized her from the previous morning as the girl who had gotten into the gray sedan.

"Well, well, David, you naughty boy, you." Rhychard watched as the Jeep faded from sight. The bronze-skinned lady clacked out of sight, her heels punching the sidewalk. *Had she been wearing the same outfit?*

So, David was cheating on his wife with street girls. Was that enough to give Vargas the entry onto Sacred Ground? Rhychard still wasn't sure how everything worked. It seemed there was a lot of gray between the Way and the Void and he was never really sure where the line was that crossed you over from one side to the other. Most people he knew were middle of the road types. They lived their lives without ever stepping into a church except for weddings or funerals. They didn't strive to do good deeds, but they didn't go around stealing or killing people, either. They survived.

Rhychard hopped back onto his Suzuki and then stopped before starting it. Sliding back off, he walked over to where his coffee cup had landed and scooped it up, folding it into a flat square, so it would fit into his back pocket. Who knew where the line was? He wasn't taking a chance that littering was it.

He swung his leg back over his bike, hit the switch and revved the throttle. Miles had not given him any answers. Renny had just given him a solid reaming. David had only given him something to gossip about, except Rhychard had no one to gossip with. *Face it, Warrior. You have nothing.* He pulled out into the flow of traffic and cranked it up. The sun was setting on the work week in a purple and orange haze leaving Harbor City in shadows. The weekend was here, but for some reason Rhychard doubted he would get to enjoy it.

I need a drink.

Eight

There were few places Rhychard enjoyed. Renny and he had never been ones to go out clubbing, preferring quiet dinners and cuddling up on the couch to an old Cary Grant movie or attending a jazz concert in the park. Common Grounds was one of his sanctuaries. The other was a quiet cigar lounge called Embers that overlooked the river. It was a small place with a leather and mahogany bar, plush chairs and couches and a walk-in humidor. There were two televisions, one showing sports and the other news, and the channels rarely changed. A balcony held small tables with metal chairs for those who wanted a view of the river while enjoying the cool evening breeze.

At least, that was normally how it was done. However, this Friday night the Florida weather decided to drop a deluge of rain upon the inhabitants of the East Coast. Rhychard darted in, using his jacket to try and cover his head, but barely succeeding. He bought a Rocky Patel and a Jameson before sliding out the back to stand under the overhang and enjoy the serenity of the storm. He had the wooden deck to himself as most of the small gathering of clientele preferred the dryness of the indoors. He needed the quietness; time alone with his thoughts.

Things were not as they should be, even more than what had become normal for him. First off, demons don't go to church. The two just weren't good for each other. He took a deep pull from the cigar as he contemplated what Vargas would need a church for. Why risk being turned to ash? He supposed it could be a perfect front for a demon operation. Who would ever suspect a church of committing evil? They had their share of hypocrisy, of course. There were always stories of pastors having affairs, money being embezzled, and even the religious phonies that manipulated the people for their own pockets. Adrian wasn't one of those pastors, however. He was lifting his cigar to his mouth again when he stopped. *Could it be a front?* That would mean there had been drastic changes to the Sacred Ground.

No. He had attended there for over two years. Those people had not been evil hiding behind a wooden cross. At least, not the ones he had met. Some were genuine such as Tim Rinehart who was always doing home repairs for the widows or Peter Locke who would take in wayward people until they got back on their feet again. How could they have turned from the Way? It didn't make sense.

The pummeling rain transformed into a mere leaky faucet as he stood in the dark. Florida weather was fickle like that. No commitment. Rhychard took a long pull from his Rocky Patel and stared at the churning river. Small whitecaps floated across the rough water, decorating the surface.

:It always seems more peaceful after a storm.:

:Isn't it a little wet for you to be padding around?: Rhychard smiled as he heard the voice reaching out to him. It had taken him quite awhile to get used to someone being in his head the way Kree was. The elven hound was privy to what went on in Rhychard's mind even though Kree promised he never invaded his privacy. The Warrior tried to trust in that, but it hadn't been easy. Now, he only slightly jumped when Kree's words suddenly blared into his head. Luckily, the coshey didn't scream like Rhychard's parents. Rhychard would have a never-ending migraine if he did.

:The rain is a good way to bathe.:

:Well, make sure you're dry before going home. I don't need the apartment to reek of wet dog.: Rhychard could feel the hound above him, more than likely on the roof. He also heard the mental version of an "hmpf."

:I am not a dog, thank you very much. Why must you always insult me?:

"Rhychard, hey, there you are. Why are you out in the rain?" Trace had opened the door and peeked out. It was obvious he was surprised to see his friend in the inclement weather.

:Because you're cute when you're insulted and you could use some cuteness in your life.: Rhychard flicked the ashes from his cigar as he turned to Trace. "Because it's quiet." He turned away from his friend and back to the rough water. He wasn't ready to forgive Trace for screwing him out of money. Not yet, anyway.

It was evident that the shaggy looking man felt the cold shoulder. He came out the rest of the way onto the patio, not worried about the drizzling rain as he was already soaked. He didn't drive often, so Rhychard assumed the other man had ridden his bike. "I saw your motorcycle out front. I wanted to give you this." He held out a couple of folded bills. "It's only forty, but I promise I'll get you the rest."

Rhychard glanced down at the cash, then back up to his friend. Trace looked like a small child trying to make amends to an older brother. Rhychard sighed as a wave of guilt washed over him. "Keep it. We're square. You did what you thought was best." He tried to sound positive, but doubted it was working.

:He is attempting to make things right, Warrior.:

:I know.: It still didn't soothe his anger at being manipulated by the man. He had had enough of that with the faerie world that had taken over his life.

"Look, I know I should have been upfront with you about the job." He shrugged. "I just thought you'd want to do something for her." He was looking everywhere but at Rhychard.

The sad part was that before he was thrust into service for the Guardian, he probably would have helped. Yet, he knew what helping people did now. It ruined your life. "Look, Trace, that thing with Captain Relco was just timing." Bad timing. A reporter had caught wind of what was going on and had been following the police captain. When Rhychard pulled John Relco out of a building before it exploded, the reporter saw it and the next thing Rhychard knew, his picture was in the paper. Luckily, the reporter didn't see the battle with the dark elves inside the warehouse. That would have been harder to explain. As further luck would have it, the captain was knocked unconscious and never saw the Unseelie that the Warrior was fighting. Rhychard was dubbed a hero, but still left alone with his secret. "My life has been crap since then and I'm done with the whole Good Samaritan bit. I'm sorry."

Trace nodded. "I get it. Really. I'm sorry. I just felt bad for the old lady."

"So do I, but there's nothing I can do." He went to take a sip from his Jameson but froze as he felt Kree mentally tighten. *:What's wrong?:*

:Gargoyles.:

:Where?: Couldn't he have just one night of relaxation without the underworld coming to ruin it?

He felt Kree rise and move off to the west. *:They gather where the Warrior Jamairlo was slain. They draw power from that victory. Vargas uses it to show them that if they can kill an Elven Warrior of the Way then a puny human should be no hindrance to them.:*

:Puny human?:

:Their words, not mine.:

Rhychard looked down at his half-enjoyed cigar and sighed. He had at least been able to enjoy six out of the twelve dollars that he spent. "I have to go," he told Trace. "There are no hard feelings. I promise." He tossed the cigar and downed the rest of his drink, setting the glass on a nearby table. He knew he needed to go after the gargoyles. Jamairlo sacrificed his life to protect the human world and Rhychard owed it to the elf not to allow his memory to be used by the Void. Evil could sure ruin a perfectly good Friday night.

"Where are you going?" Trace stared, confused.

Rhychard couldn't blame him. His life confused him, as well. "There's something I have to check on, that's all. I'll reach out to you tomorrow." Trace just said okay as Rhychard passed back through Embers and out the front door.

The bar was close to Downtown where Jamairlo was slain, so Rhychard followed Kree's path, minus the rooftop part. The rain ceased, leaving the city in a blanket of puddles and dripping trees. It was morbid to him that people, even gargoyles, would continue to huddle around a place of death. He understood leaving flowers and such, but to hang out on the side of the road and just stand around had too much of the macabre in it for him. He would rather celebrate life than death. Of course, the Void would use any means to gain strength from a victory over the Way.

:There are only three. However, they seem more intent on watching a young lady walking the street.:

:What is she doing?:

:Vomiting.:

:Is she drunk?: Rhychard supposed creatures of darkness had to get their entertainment somehow. They probably didn't have cable television in the Nether and Vargas was too cheap to spring for it in his evil lair. Did demons even have lairs? Or was that strictly a comic book thing? He still had so much to learn about these types of things.

:I think not. She was getting out of a car just as I was arriving. The vehicle drove away and the lady immediately relieved her stomach of its contents. A Whopper, I surmise.:

:I don't need a detailed description. That was just disgusting, you know that?: Rhychard heard a loud screech and then he was slammed into the ground, pain slicing his shoulder. As soon as he hit the concrete he rolled to the right, hoping it was the smart choice. He came up quickly and reached for the handle of the Guardian Sword that was always there. Voices

of a dozen Warriors wailed for vengeance. The glamour fell away as he drew it, slicing through the air at where he thought he heard the beating of wings. The beast screamed as Rhychard's blades severed its left arm and buried itself into the creature's side, shattering its ribs. With a death screech the beast exploded in a ball of ash.

"Why can't they just vanish in a puff of smoke?" Rhychard wiped gargoyle remains from his jacket sleeve.

:At least it's not blood and guts.: Kree mind-spoke. *:Heads up, Warrior. The others are coming.:*

:Great.: Rhychard looked around, but no one else was in sight. Good. He didn't need witnesses. He sheathed the Guardian Sword, silencing the voices and pulled out his two short swords instead. Glancing up at the roof, he saw Kree squatting as close to the darkened Spanish tiles as he could get. With any luck he could take out one of the flying bats in a surprise attack.

The first two flew past Kree's hiding spot, directly toward Rhychard. As the third gargoyle drew closer, Kree leaped, his growl echoing from the surrounding buildings. His massive paws out, he caught the beast by the left wing and dug in with his claws. The creature shrieked, spinning out of control. Kree swung his hind legs to the creature's stomach and slashed out, ripping the gargoyle open. A shriek, a puff of ash and Kree was tumbling to the ground in a cloud of gargoyle remains, sneezing.

The first gargoyle kept his fix on Rhychard while the second stopped in mid-flight and turned to face Kree who had landed on his feet in the middle of the street. Rhychard tossed his short sword in the air slightly, catching it like a javelin and launched it. The first gargoyle dodged. The second, however, didn't see it coming. It plunged into his back between his wings and he was gone. Ash and sword fell to the ground.

The remaining gargoyle slowed, flittering around in a small square. He jerked his head back and forth, first looking at the Warrior, then at the coshey. The odds were *not* in his favor. With a loud yowl at the sky, he darted up and out of sight.

Rhychard watched him go, his fist tight around his sword, his breathing heavy. Once the creature was out of sight, he walked over to retrieve his fallen blade and asked if Kree was all right.

:They reek worse than damp dog.:

"Agreed." Rhychard glanced to where the girl should have been as he slid the swords over his shoulder and into their holsters. They vanished as soon as he released the pommels.

:She left once the fighting commenced, but I don't think she heard anything.:

Rhychard nodded. Why would gargoyles be following a girl who worked the streets? Wasn't she already a child of the Void?

:That's not how it works, Warrior. Motives not actions. Her business is to bring pleasure to her clients and she does that with her body. How is that different than people who bring pleasure by their music or art? Just because your human society believes something is wrong doesn't mean that the Way does. On the contrary, quite often those who would protest what she does and wish to bring harm to her to make her cease her business are of the Void. Do you really think that those who would blow up abortion clinics are of the Way? Your world sometimes has a skewed view of the righteous path.:

"No arguments there, my friend." Rhychard walked over to Kree and ran his hand along the elven hound's back, the fur still damp but now coated with ash. "I think we both need a bath."

Kree shook his coat, ash flying off of him. *:Agreed.:*

Nine

Saturday morning arrived way too early as far as Rhychard was concerned. He rolled over onto his side and tried to focus on the digital clock sitting on the television tray he used as a nightstand. 12:07. All right, he thought as he flopped back onto his back, noon came way too early.

He opened and shut his eyes a few times chasing away sleep as he coaxed his body into a sitting position. From the foot of his bed, he heard the familiar mixture of air popping and jingling bells. "Rhychard, come quick!" Tryna vanished as soon as she finished speaking.

Rhychard stared at the vacant spot wondering if she was going to come back and tell him where "here" was.

:Warrior, to the park with haste!: Kree's voice sounded strained. *:Gargoyles attack!:*

Rhychard hurled himself out of the twin bed and shoved himself into clothes. He snatched his harness of short swords along with the Guardian Sword with one hand, sliding it over his arms and strapping them onto his back. At the same time, he grabbed his brace of knives and his coat while making for the door. Matters were worse than he thought if gargoyles were out while the sun was hottest. Creatures of the night usually stuck to the night, or so the stereotype went. Life would be easier if lived with the stereotypes. Then, the players would be obvious and predictable. Predictable was good. Predictable made his life easy. Gargoyles used to be predictable. Now, they were just annoying.

Jerking the door open, he skipped the steps and dropped to the sidewalk running, the sun screaming at his sleepy eyes. The park was three blocks from his condo and Rhychard ran the whole way, his coat flapping behind him like a cape. *Batman, eat your heart out.* As the noon brightness stung his eyes, he wished he had grabbed his sunglasses. *I should keep them in my coat.*

Mark Shephard Park was named after a fifteen-year-old boy who had lost his battle with cancer several years ago. His family had donated an obscene amount of money to have the park cleaned up and enhanced. To the east were swing sets, slides and a fort shaped like a pirate ship. To the west sat a few small picnic pavilions and one large pavilion where forty people could barbecue on any given weekend—for a small deposit, that is. Over the years, street girls would bring their dates to the park to do business, and cops had taken to driving through at night rousting parked cars and flashing their blinding search lights.

Rhychard slowed and glanced around looking for a battle, but both the playground and the tables were empty. *Where are they?*

:To the lake in the back, Warrior! Hurry! They almost have her.:

Rhychard sprinted to the man-made lake at the back of the park. He reached over his shoulder as he ran and drew both short swords, not needing the voices in his head that came with the Guardian Sword. They materialized as he gripped them in his hands, pulling them out in front of him. Kree would never lie to him about gargoyles.

And he hadn't.

Six of the flying beasts flew circles around a young lady, diving at her with their claws extended, lashing out. The lady tried to take refuge in the lake where she now thrashed around, water spraying everywhere. Stupid. Now, the leathery creatures were trying to drown her as well as rip her asunder. Kree was leaping at them as they came within reach, rising up on his hind legs and striking out with his paws, which made Rhychard's hands look like a newborn's. The coshey was kicking up so much water he was almost drowning the girl he was trying to save, which really didn't matter since the girl was almost drowning herself.

Tryna was popping in and out, using a small dirk to slash at the gargoyles whenever she reappeared near one. She was more of a distraction to the creatures than a threat as their hides were too thick for her small weapon. Still, Rhychard thought, if she could get that point into an eye, she could very well blind one. He communicated his idea to Kree and asked him to relay it to Tryna.

:She said she will try.:

That's all he could ask.

Rhychard slashed at the nearest gargoyle with a backward swing as he neared the lake. :*Kree, try and get the woman to me.:* The elven hound leaped into the air, water showering everything within yards, his massive jaws open revealing jagged teeth about as long as Rhychard's ring fingers.

As Kree started to fall back to the water, his jaws clamped down on one of the gargoyle's legs, dragging it down with him. The dark creature beat his wings frantically trying to stay out of the water, but to no avail. Kree bit down harder and jerked his head to the right severing the leg from the gargoyle. The creature shrieked as greenish fluid oozed from the wound and then the gargoyle vanished in a shower of gray ash.

Five left.

Rhychard crisscrossed his short swords in front of him as two of the gargoyles attacked at his approach. Kree spit out the ash of the severed limb and was herding the girl toward the lake shore. All Rhychard could see of her was honey skin and long, dark hair. He heard another shriek and turned to see Tryna pulling her dirk from a gargoyle's lemony eye. The creature clawed at the ruined eye, howling in pain. Rhychard took a back swing at one of the creature's attacking him, then drove his sword into the ground, reached for one of his knives and threw it at Tryna's victim. The blade lodged in the creature's chest and then gargoyle and knife were gone, the gargoyle disappearing in a cloud of ash while the knife fell into the water below.

"Dammit!" Rhychard yelled at himself. "That was one of my good knives." He picked up his sword and swung it at a descending gargoyle, slicing through the creature's thick neck.

Three left.

The girl, Latino descent now that Rhychard could see her, was crawling out of the lake onto the grassy shore. Something about her seemed familiar, but Rhychard couldn't get a good look at her. Kree was staying close to the woman, his massive frame dwarfing her huddled form. It was like looking at a baby with a lion. Tryna popped into the air below one of the gargoyles and shoved upward where the beast's genitals would be. Did gargoyles even have genitals? Regardless, it was a weak spot and the blade sank into the creature. Both Tryna and the blade poofed out of sight again, followed shortly by the dead gargoyle.

Rhychard held his swords in front of him. Two left.

He stood, braced, swords pointing outward. The remaining two gargoyles forgot the girl, obviously realizing that the threat he posed was greater than their attack on the girl. One flew up, the other down, both focused intently on Rhychard. So much so in fact that they forgot Kree's reach and the one flying low came within distance of the elven hound's massive paws. Kree leaped, batting at the gargoyle almost like a cat would a toy, and knocked it toward Rhychard. The Warrior brought the sword in his right hand into a back swing slicing into the creature's chest. With a howl that echoed across the water, there was only one gargoyle left.

The black, leather-hide creature hesitated for only a moment before it turned and flew off across the lake. Rhychard watched it leave until the black dot winked out of sight. When the sky was clear of trouble, Rhychard bent to the grass and wiped the greenish muck that passed for gargoyle blood off his blades. Reaching over his shoulders, he slid the blades back into the harness. As soon as he released the hilts, the swords vanished.

Tryna popped back with her tinkling melody and knelt beside the fallen girl. Kree sat on his back haunches, tongue lolling and tail beating a steady rhythm on the grass as he took up guard duty over the girl. *:Our mystery deepens, Warrior.:*

Rhychard lifted his brows as he looked from the coshey to Tryna, her tiny hands on the woman's arm and forehead. Tryna's eyes were closed and he could hear the musical hum that told him she was using her powers to examine the girl. When he finally got close enough to see the woman they had rescued, he froze. *What the hell?*

Rhychard had to force his mouth to close as he stared down into the face of the girl they had rescued the night before, as well. *:What do the gargoyles want with a street hooker?:*

:A question of some complexity, for sure.: Kree sent him.

There was no doubt in Rhychard's mind what the lady did for a living. Even if he hadn't seen her getting in and out of cars the past couple of days, her choice of clothing revealed all, literally. Her "fuck me" pumps had laces tied up to her calves. Her face was caked with paint that he supposed was intended to look appealing to somebody. She wore a flimsy spaghetti strap blouse that revealed her ample breasts, the nipples poking hard at the wet fabric and a short skirt that could hardly be called a skirt since it barely covered anything. By the curves of her ass exposed to the afternoon sun, Rhychard could tell panties were an obstacle she did without. This woman, whoever she was, was dressed for work, the kind that took place in cars parked in dark alleys, not the business district. So, why had gargoyles tried twice to kill her?

"Well?" Rhychard squatted down beside Tryna, his eyes taking in all he could of the girl on the ground.

Tryna sat back on her heels, her hands on her thighs, eyelids fluttering open. "She fainted, but seems all right considering. Cold and wet, obviously." Tryna took a deep breath and stood to her feet. "We need to get her somewhere safe. Shall we take her back to your place?"

The Warrior glanced down at the unconscious girl. Her soaking sheer shirt stuck to her drenched body, the fabric tight against her breasts. "Can't you just pop her there?"

Tryna's hands went to her hips as her eyes narrowed, which was kind of comical considering she was only two and a half feet tall and model thin. "You know very well that I can't." Her words were like icicles. "If you weren't trying so hard to look like some cult television show, you'd already have her in your arms."

Kree made a mental noise that Rhychard could only take as a laugh.

"Thanks, mutt."

:No need to be insulting.:

Rhychard leaned down, slid a hand under her back and one under her knees and then lifted. He was amazed at how light she was. The bumps of her spine dug into his forearm and her legs were chopsticks. He held her so that her head rested on his chest and started the walk back to his condo, her weight almost negligible. Tryna said she'd meet them there and then poofed out of sight with her musical accompaniment. Kree stood and followed him, padding silently beside him.

Rhychard wondered what water would do to his coat.

Ten

Rhychard took a long drag from his cigar, held the smoke a moment and then exhaled slowly, sending smoke ribbons over the porch railing. It was his favorite place in the apartment and the only place not covered in left-behind fur. It was odd having a roommate that shed, but Rhychard would take that over blaring rap music any day. His last roommate had been a disaster, and he was more than pleased that nightmare had ended.

When he entered his apartment, Rhychard had deposited the still unconscious girl on his bed and left her in Tryna's tiny, but capable, hands. Kree had merely taken over the couch, as always, head resting on one arm, feet dangling off the other. The faerie was probably the least intimidating of the three of them, even being a creature over six hundred years old.

The fact that gargoyles tried to rip the girl apart and in broad daylight, a pretty bold move on their part, bothered Rhychard. Of course, creatures of the Void didn't care if they were seen by humans as it only enhanced the fear they fed on. The faerie world, however, was more discreet, wishing to be anonymous to the world above and out of the public eye. Kendalais had scolded him severely when the reporter captured a picture of him. "A Warrior does not draw attention to himself, and yet, here you are like some human celebrity. It is not how it is done."

"How was I to know the captain was being followed? I was watching for dark elves and gargoyles. You didn't tell me to keep an eye out for humans, as well." Rhychard had been fuming. Having his picture in the paper had been the last thing he wanted and the pompous elf accused him of doing it on purpose.

"It is a Warrior's job to know everything. How can you protect John Relco if you do not know everything that is going on around him? How are you to protect your world if you are not diligent in your observation of your surroundings? A Warrior uses his senses. Taste your environment. Feel your surroundings. Hear the very wind around you and allow it to speak to you."

All Rhychard could think was that he had left the world of *Buffy the Vampire Slayer* and entered *Karate Kid* with a pointy eared Mr. Miyagi. At the time, all he wanted to do was "wax on and wax off" the Warrior Master's sneer. He had been like that since the first night he appeared in Rhychard's old apartment. He wore his arrogance like cheap cologne and it took everything for Rhychard to get the narcissistic stench out of his nostrils.

Kendalais entered his life three days after Jamairlo had died and left him with the Guardian Sword and cryptic talk of being chosen and a destiny. For three days, Rhychard paced his apartment with the sword hidden between his mattress and box springs. For three days, he turned down work and avoided seeing Renny or his family, waiting for some creature from a Stephen King novel to bust in on him and rip him apart. He didn't eat. He didn't sleep. He didn't even shower. He sat in the middle of the room and stared at the front door. If it had been humans after him, he would not be so scared, but these creatures were anything but human.

On the third day, exhaustion had drained him and he had fallen asleep in his easy chair. He didn't know how long he had been out, because he had ceased looking at clocks. The only reason he woke at all was because of the hairs on the back of his neck tingling so bad he knew, even in his slumber, he wasn't alone. From a dead sleep, Rhychard jumped awake and out of the recliner, his heart pounding, his breathing ragged gasps.

Kendalais stood there, his arms crossed over his powerful chest and his left eyebrow cocked over eyes that shimmered the bright blue of clear, shallow ocean water. He had long blond hair that fell to the middle of his back and his pointed ears poked their way through the thin strands. Another elf. Only this one was in armor and wore a gold cloak with a cowl that he wasn't using to hide his appearance. Attached to a thick leather belt was a sword whose pommel matched the one Jamairlo had given Rhychard. Or maybe it was the sword itself. What if the elf in front of him had used some magical GPS and found the hiding place and already took possession of the blade.

"You found the sword, I see." Rhychard pointed at the blade at Kendalais's side. "Good, good. Glad you did."

"This is my sword, not the one in your possession." The elf actually sounded bored. "That one, I am afraid, is yours."

"Mine?"

The elf narrowed his eyes at Rhychard. "Do you have a hearing defect?"

"No. Why?"

"Then you heard me say that the sword is yours. Why repeat it?"

"I meant, why is it mine? You must be confused. The sword belongs to an elf."

Kendalais sighed. "Why it is yours escapes me, but nevertheless, it is. And I am never confused about such things. The Guardian of the Way has deemed it proper for you to replace Jamairlo as Warrior of this area. It is beyond me to understand such matters."

"Well, if you're not here to take it back, why are you here?"

"It seems I am to be punished for some past evil on my part, although I have no idea as to what I have done to deserve such a fate." The elf glanced heavenward as if expecting an answer to the mystery. When he received none, he sighed and turned his sneer back to Rhychard. "I am Kendalais, Sidhe Warrior Master of the Seelie. I have been sent here to begin your training as a Warrior of the Way and assist you in completing Jamairlo's task."

"You mean the task that got him eaten by those giant bats? Forget it." Rhychard waved his arms back and forth in front of him as he turned and circled the recliner, trying to put something between him and what Kendalais was saying. "You can have the sword back and be on your merry little way."

The elf didn't move. "You seem to be under the misguided understanding that I want to be here. I assure you, I do not. I find the fact that the Guardian chose a human to replace a great elven Warrior to be insulting and contemptible. The fact that I have to train you merely adds to the injustice of it all. Be that as it may, however, neither you nor I have a choice in the matter. We are merely here to do the Guardian's bidding."

"No, we're not. You are. I want nothing to do with it. Any of it."

"As I said and which you make me repeat, I wish it were so, but it's not. The Guardian chooses who he will and, may fate spare us, he has chosen a human. You."

Rhychard found he was pacing again. None of it was making sense. Guardian. Swords. Elves. He walked to the back of his apartment and stared out the window. He had gone crazy. That was all there was to it. No one was going to believe him. Hell, he didn't believe him. He took a few deep breaths to try and calm his nerves, but it didn't help. What was he going to tell Renny?

"I understand that all of this is more than your human brain can comprehend, but we do not have time for you to ponder your fate. John Relco is in danger and the Destroyer is trying to have him killed. We must protect him."

Rhychard recognized the name from Jamairlo, but didn't know who it was. He wasn't sure he wanted to know. The last time he helped someone his world exploded. He ran his hand through his long hair. He just wanted all of this to go away.

"I will allow you tonight to contemplate the truth of things. Tomorrow, I will return and we will begin your sword training as I assume you have not used one before the other night. Tryna will be the one to help you understand your importance in this."

Rhychard just sighed and shook his head. As he turned to tell the elf he was off his rocker, the seven-foot, pointy eared freak was gone. He just stared at the empty spot where Kendalais had been a moment earlier, wondering how the elf had gotten in or out of the apartment and just who the hell Tryna was. Or, as things were going so far, what she was.

Rhychard had tried to put his life back on a normal track. He had called Renny and apologized for his disappearing act with a lie made up of work and illness. She pretended to buy it, but he could tell she believed there was more to the story than he was letting on. She had trusted him that much. At least, in the beginning of the nightmare she had. It had only grown worse as he had to constantly break dates and vanish without a word. In order to keep her out of what was happening, he had built a silent wall between them. He did his best to keep up normal appearances, to shield her from what was happening to him, but eventually the wall was insurmountable and what was his life was lost.

It was not going to return to normal, either. Rhychard stared out at the woods behind his condo as he let go of his thoughts of the past. He was stuck in some bizarre fantasy world and his only thought was how to protect Renny from the chaos that was swallowing him.

He had done a lousy job of it, so far. Not only was she gone from his life, wanting nothing to do with him, but now, three months later, those very creatures he had wanted to protect her from had made her a target. Why they were after her, he had no idea. He had to figure it out, though, and fix it. He owed it to her to save her, even if she didn't realize she needed saving.

:Warrior, the girl wakes. Tryna says for you to come.:

Rhychard set his cigar on the ashtray that he kept on the railing, took one last look at the beautiful eastern sky and went inside. Kree was still on the couch, muzzle resting on his massive paws. "Taking it easy, I see."

:Tryna thinks my appearance might frighten the girl's fragile state of mind.:

"You scare me and I've known you for a couple of months."

:This critical side of you is rather droll.:

Rhychard rolled his eyes. He lived with an over-sized dog who spoke as if he lived in a literary magazine. "What has Tryna found out about our friendly neighborhood street girl?"

:That she was switching sides and Vargas wasn't happy about it. She calls herself Buttercup and somehow she is tied into that plastic preacher of the church we found you at yesterday.:

Rhychard passed through the living room, into the hall, and into the apartment's master bedroom. He assumed it was the master bedroom since it was the biggest. It was also his bedroom, and since he was master of the house that seemed to make it the master bedroom. He loved his logic.

Tryna sat on the bed, legs crisscrossed in front of her, forearms resting on her knees, hands clasped. The girl they had rescued—Buttercup—was sitting up, her back hard against the wall at the head of the bed. She was wearing one of Rhychard's Florida State Jerseys as her sodden clothes had been stripped off her by Tryna and put in the dryer by Rhychard. From swashbuckling hero to laundry man, all in one afternoon. The over-abundance of makeup had also been somewhat pressure washed off of the young woman, leaving her face a pasty color and he could now see chocolate brown eyes lost inside hollow sockets. Her lips were pressed into a thin line almost turning them white. She was scared and he didn't blame her.

"Hello there, Rhychard," Tryna said without looking at him. "This young lady you have loaned your bed to is Buttercup."

He put on his most charming smile as he took a spot close, but not threateningly close, to the young girl and leaned against the white wall. "And my college Jersey. Hopefully you're not a Gator fan."

"Never was much of one to keep up with college sports," she said with a limp smile.

Rhychard nodded his head. "I am sure you had other things to worry about."

"Like survival," Tryna said.

Rhychard glanced at the small faerie. Her back was flagpole straight and her index fingers kept up a steady drumming on her knees. She was definitely wound tight. Tryna knew what Rhychard was about to find out and, apparently, she didn't like it.

"A pretty scary morning," Rhychard said. "Have you ever seen gargoyles before?"

Buttercup gave him a puzzled look. "Gargoyles? Like in the Disney show? They're real?"

Rhychard nodded. "Many things people don't think are real are real." And he gestured to Tryna with his chin.

"I saw that."

He smiled. "And most are magical, of sorts."

Tryna glanced over at him and he could tell she wanted to make some smartass comment but didn't. He just smiled at her some more.

"Why were they after me?" Buttercup folded in on herself, her hands rubbing up and down on her upper arms. She was scared. She had a right to be.

"Well, I can only guess, but I'd say you've made some life changing decisions lately," Rhychard said. "Gargoyles are servants of the Void, what you would call evil. My guess would be you were living your life in a way that honored or served the Void and recently have made a decision that would have put you on the path of the Way, which, basically, you would call good. The Void hates losing members, but then again, what religion doesn't. The Void's exit plan, however, is a little drastic"

Buttercup glared at the Warrior. "I am not evil."

Tryna reached out and brushed the hair from the girl's eyes. "No, sweetheart, you are not."

"Nevertheless, you were living for the Void," Rhychard said, ignoring Tryna's icy glare. "You may not have shed blood or practiced occult sacrifices, but you were living your life for the Void, regardless."

:Your bedside manner leaves a lot to be desired,: Kree's voice sounded in his head. Rhychard ignored him. No one took it easy on him when he discovered faerie tales were real and he saw no reason to sugarcoat things with this girl he had seen climbing out of David Morsetti's Jeep.

"Look, Buttercup, forget what you know of religion, most of it is superstition anyway. Think of life in terms of good and evil, not actions, but motives. A man kills another man to steal his money. That's evil. Now, say a man shoots and kills someone to protect his family. That's not evil, even though the act is the same. Motive makes an act evil or good. That's the basic difference between the Way and the Void. You did something that changed your motives and Vargas sent the gargoyles after you."

The girl stared at the bed with her chocolate eyes. She still had that deer-in-the-headlights look about her. Rhychard couldn't blame her. Gargoyles attacked her, a sword fight saved her, and a coshey and a faerie girl had found her. None of it was exactly your normal day for a hooker.

"I'm evil because I'm a…because of what I did?"

"Motive, not action," Rhychard repeated, a finger in the air. "And you just said 'did,' so I'm assuming you've decided against that as a career choice. Why were you in the park today?"

Buttercup closed her eyes as guilt painted her face like a Mardi Gras mask. She stretched her arms out in front of her, rubbing at the bed nervously with her fingers. Her voice when it came was a whisper. "Adrian said he needed to talk to me one more time. We were supposed to meet there, by the picnic tables."

"Adrian? You mean Pastor Adrian?"

At first, Buttercup didn't say anything. She just sat there staring at her hands as she twirled her fingers around in agitated nervousness. Or was it fear? Neither Rhychard nor Tryna said a word, giving her space and time. Finally, the honey-skinned girl nodded.

Tryna turned and glanced at Rhychard, the confusion he felt revealing itself on her face. What was a pastor meeting a prostitute in the middle of the day for? "Were you and he…um…well, you know? Was he a client?" He took a deep breath, not sure where his sudden shyness came from. It was obviously this girl's profession. Why was he embarrassed?

She shook her head. "Not really. At least, not for himself."

"He pimped you out?"

"No, it was worse than that." Buttercup then went on to describe how she helped Adrian acquire blackmail photos on different people who were obstacles to his goals. It ranged from people within his church who were against him to city officials he needed special favors from. That explained how he had acquired all of that land so cheap as well as the speed in which the buildings went up. He was blackmailing people with photos of them cheating on their wives in order to clear the way for whatever he wanted, and it didn't matter if they never had sex with Buttercup. The pictures made it seem like they had and the men weren't willing to take the chance that people wouldn't believe them. Of course, that explained why Adrian was doing it, but what was in it for Vargas? There had to be more than just being able to desecrate Sacred Ground.

And what did it have to do with Renny?

"What was the meeting about today?" Other than a set up to kill the poor girl, that is.

Buttercup shook her head. "I don't know. I had stopped doing his dirty work." Tears welled up in her dark eyes as she spoke. "I saw what it was doing to those men. Some had refused to be blackmailed and they lost their jobs, sometimes their families. I climbed into some guy's Jeep last night and he didn't even wink at me. He tried to convince me to get off the street. Even offered to help. Here he is trying to *save* me and all I could think about was someone had taken pictures of him and I and were going to use them to hurt him. I couldn't do it anymore. It was making me sick. I called Adrian last night and told him just that. He said he understood and that there were other girls who would love to make the money he was paying me."

"Poor girl," Tryna said, patting the other's hand. "You know the truth. He can't allow you to tell someone else."

Buttercup's head jerked up, the tears flowing freely now. "But I promised I wouldn't. I just wanted out. I wouldn't have told anyone. As it was Jerome got pissed and knocked me around. I thought perhaps this morning was to force me to do that shit some more"

"Who is Jerome?" Tryna asked.

"Her pimp, I would guess." Rhychard just shrugged. "If Adrian couldn't convince you to keep doing his dirty deeds, then he couldn't take a chance that you went to the cops. The untrustworthy don't trust very easy, themselves."

:Vargas must have control of Adrian,: Kree mind-spoke.

Buttercup's eyes went wide as she started backing toward the wall. She would have gone through it if she could. Her head jerked this way and that in search of the person who spoke. "Who's here? Who said that?"

:Good job you giant Chihuahua. You had to pick right then to go public with your sneaky voice?: Rhychard shook his head. "That was Kree. The horse of a dog that helped us save you today. He's harmless."

:Chihuahua? Horse of a dog? You, dear sir, are rude.:

"How come I can hear him?" She was plastered so hard against the drywall, Rhychard was sure she'd leave a permanent indention.

"Kree is a coshey," Tryna said. "He comes from the same place as me."

"And no one knows where that is," Rhychard said. "He speaks to people in their minds. It's part of his magic. Kree's right, though. That may explain why Vargas can get onto church property."

:I wonder what's there that he wants,: the coshey said.

Eleven

It was a very good question. Outside of conquering an establishment of the Way and desecrating Sacred Ground, Vargas seemed way too hungry for Harvest Fellowship for there not to be something else motivating him. Rhychard tied his long black hair into a ponytail with a leather thong, donned his long coat over his swords, and left the others in his apartment. Buttercup had calmed down but only after Tryna put an enchantment on her to make her sleep. He still wasn't sure what to do with her. As soon as she reappeared on the street the gargoyles would be after her. She was a liability to whatever Adrian and Vargas were scheming.

All across Harbor City the nine-to-five types were making the most out of their weekend. They had traded their suits and ties for shorts and flip flops as they made their way to parks and malls. The late August air was chilly as it kicked up mini tornadoes sending leaves and discarded candy wrappers into a swirling frenzy. Rhychard allowed his jacket to flap behind him as he glided his crotch rocket through weekend traffic, ignoring the horns and fingers that went up in his wake. The wind whipped past him as he sliced his way through the city, his thoughts on Harvest Fellowship, Pastor Adrian, and the demon, Vargas. An unholy alliance if ever there was one. Yet, he was sure that it had happened throughout history. Churches and temples weren't always Sacred Ground. The Crusades were a devastating period of history when the Void almost tipped the balance. However, it was the same in any religion. Modern day terrorists used their faith as a justification for evil. Yet, most in Islam were of the Way and lived righteous lives. *A few rotten apples,* Rhychard thought as he leaned into a tight right turn.

That part of his learning to be a Warrior of the Way had been easy to comprehend. Even when he had joined Renny at Harvest Fellowship he had a hard time swallowing the details of what they were preaching. However, he had always had a strong sense of right and wrong. It was that mindset that caused him to leave his moving truck that night when he heard Jamairlo's scream. Someone was in trouble and he had to help. Walking away just wouldn't have been…right. Still, if he had known it was going to change his life he may have forced himself to drive on.

No, even then he would have followed his gut and went to help. Except, it wasn't his gut entirely that made him rush headlong into a batch of pissed off gargoyles. The Guardian had played tag with his will and pushed Rhychard into that mess. He had been called, according to Tryna. If he had been able to ignore the call, then he wouldn't have been chosen in the first place. It was his sense of right and wrong that caused him to answer the Guardian's summons.

The right and wrong part had been easy to grasp. What had been difficult was being faced with faeries and elves. When Jamairlo shoved the Guardian Sword into his hand, his blond hair falling back to reveal pointy ears and slanted brows, Rhychard had almost been too frozen in place to save his own life. Of course, gargoyles flying down to rip your head from your shoulders is enough to spur you to action. He had to have looked like a scared child swinging the blade like a baseball bat or club rather than a sword. Still, it worked. He survived.

Jamairlo had not, however, at least not for long. The elf gave him the sword, making him promise to protect it until someone showed up for it. At that point, Rhychard had been afraid of just what the elf meant by "someone." He took the sword and ran, worried about gargoyles more than cops at the moment. Once he had the sword tucked under his mattress, the only hiding spot he could think of, he sat in his easy chair, not wanting to be near a blade he had seen glow. He just stared at the door, waiting until he finally fell asleep where he sat.

Then Kendalais arrived scaring him half to death, announcing that he had been chosen to be a Warrior of the Way. He didn't want to be chosen. He just wanted to live his life and be left alone. Yet, it wasn't that easy. The sword called him, held him. Someone's life depended on him. The world needed Warriors, called by the Guardian, to keep the balance, and it didn't matter that it completely threw his life out of balance in the process. He wondered if cops had the same problem.

The day was slowly turning from noon to evening, the sun in the west beginning its descent. Rhychard's ponytail flapped behind him in the wind he was making with his motorcycle as he thought back to the days after he was given the sword. Kendalais had been true to his word. The next day he was there wearing his cloak of arrogance, ready to teach a pathetic human how to use a sword without killing himself. However, he was alone.

"Weren't you supposed to have some woman with you?" Rhychard stood with his arms crossed over his chest, his face a mask of anger. These elves had barged in on his life with plans to take it over. While he may not have had a choice in what happened to him, he could choose how he reacted to it and right then, scorn seemed to be the appropriate response.

Kendalais cocked his eyebrow at him. "Some woman? Tryna is an ellyll over six centuries in years as you would count them. The ellyll are the Keepers of Knowledge and it is she who will instruct you in the Way. I will be your trainer while she is your instructor."

"Wow, six hundred years old. She must get some senior discounts." Rhychard wasn't sure how to handle something so old or even knew what an ellyll was. While his fear began to return, he refused to show it to the pompous Sidhe. "So, where is she?"

Kendalais stared at Rhychard a moment before turning his attention to the wall. Something wasn't right. Rhychard could read it all over the elf's face and Kendalais didn't want to answer the question. "We don't know."

Now Rhychard knew why Kendalais didn't want to answer him. The elf wasn't one that enjoyed being ignorant of anything. "You don't know?" Of course, Rhychard wanted to twist any screw that made Kendalais uncomfortable. "You lost her?"

"The ellyll are a race, not possessions. You lose things, not people." He paused in his tirade and took a deep breath. He seemed genuinely concerned for whoever Tryna was, so Rhychard refrained from baiting him further. "She has taken the death of Jamairlo and Meelim very seriously. She had been his fountain of knowledge for a century and a half. His demise has struck her hard. She has gone off to be alone." He straightened, probably aware that he was showing emotion for someone else. "Enough. We need to train you with the Guardian Sword. You will need to learn how to draw on its power if you are to defeat the Void without killing yourself."

Over the next few days, Kendalais had instructed him, not only on swordsmanship, but also on the history of the sword and how to keep the souls of past Warriors from taking him over. "Its magic will protect you along with your skill. You must draw on both of them to survive and defeat your enemy."

"I don't have an enemy."

Kendalais pierced him with his cold, blue eyes. "You do now."

It didn't take long for Rhychard to discover the truth of the elf's words.

The memory scattered as Kree's question popped back into Rhychard's head at the thought of his enemies. *I wonder what's there that Vargas wants.* Creatures of the Void usually avoided Sacred Ground, so it had to be more than a taunt on the demon's part. Something had to be there, but what? Rhychard hit the throttle on his Suzuki and did a quick U-turn. It was time to have a talk with Adrian Michaels. It was Saturday, so he wasn't sure the good pastor would be there, but it was worth a visit to see. *Hopefully, it goes better than the last time I was at the church.*

As he neared the church parking lot, he noticed Adrian leaving the building, but he wasn't alone. Rhychard let go of the throttle and coasted into an office plaza across the street to wait. He didn't want to confront the pastor in front of witnesses.

Adrian Michaels was a tall man with perfectly manicured black hair and a slender, strong build. He had always worn suits, tailor made and double breasted. Not your average run-of-the-mill preacher's garb to be sure. Furthermore, he always seemed to have a tan even during the coldest months, but was rarely ever seen outdoors. *Probably has a tanning booth in his closet.* He was also always smiling, which at first inspired Rhychard, but after a while, it unnerved him. No one could be that happy all of the time. Yet, Adrian never seemed to have a bad day.

Rhychard watched as Adrian escorted the younger woman to her car. Their vehicles were the only two on the lot, which Rhychard found odd as Adrian had always preached never be alone with a member of the opposite sex unless you were married with them. They were laughing as they walked and the pastor slid his hand to the small of the woman's back. "That's not a very pastoral place to put your hand, Pastor Adrian," Rhychard said to himself. "That shows a level of intimacy."

Something about the way the woman walked seemed very familiar to Rhychard. He knew the woman, somehow. And then, he noticed her car and his throat caught as his stomach tightened. It was a hunter green Altima. Renny's car. No wonder she had become so pissed off when he asked her who she was seeing. It was a married man. And her pastor!

Adrian opened the driver's door to her car and held it as she slid behind the wheel. She had squeezed the pastor's hand before entering the vehicle, a long tight squeeze as she pushed up on her tiptoes and kissed his cheek. She smiled enough that it made Rhychard's jaws hurt. Adrian shut her door and then just stood and watched as the younger—much younger—woman drove off before he started toward his Escalade.

Rhychard wanted to vomit. It was all he could do to keep himself from racing over to Adrian and running him through with his sword. If he didn't need the man to find out what Vargas was up to, he would have made a pastor shish kabob. Instead, with a deep breath through gritted teeth, he revved his way across Hudson Street and into the perfectly landscaped parking lot of Harvest Fellowship Church. Adrian was almost to his vehicle when Rhychard pulled in front of him cutting him off.

"A little young for you, isn't she?" Rhychard said as he leaned forward on his handle bars.

Adrian Michaels paused as he made a show of buttoning his elephant gray jacket. "Rhychard, what brings you to church?" His voice smiled and it was all Rhychard could do not to punch him.

Instead, he turned his head in the direction Renny had driven off in as if he could still see her. "What does Mrs. Michaels think of your personal touch with your congregation?"

Adrian just chuckled. "Now, Rhychard, there is nothing going on between Renny and I. She's been coming for counseling since you two broke up and, for your information, Linda knows we were here together, as does my secretary who you just missed. As a matter of fact, it is because of you that she was here. She wanted to tell me about your visit at her office."

"To warn you that I was coming to church next week, I'm sure. Good thing too, so you can warn Vargas. However, I'm sure your little friend already knows. When exactly did you start working with demons, anyway?"

This time the older man laughed. "Demons? Please, Rhychard, don't tell me you actually believe in demons?"

Rhychard smiled. "You're a preacher. Isn't it your job to believe in them?"

Running his hand through his perfect hair, Adrian gave a slight shrug of his thick shoulders. "The demons of today are addictions more or less, like alcohol, sex, or drugs. They're negative personality traits like envy and greed. Demons are allegorical, Rhychard, the stuff of fantasy writers."

"Wouldn't adultery be one of those demons?" Rhychard squeezed the tank of his bike. He needed something to keep his anger in check.

Adrian sighed. "Rhychard, I am not the one who cheated on Renny."

"No, you're cheating on your wife *with* Renny. And for the record, I didn't cheat on her."

"She seems to think you did. She tells me of many nights you were out without any real reason. She also says she heard you talking with another female. Alone. You wouldn't even tell her who it was. What is she supposed to think?"

"She's supposed to trust." There were many things he couldn't tell Renny, but he never thought she would stop trusting him. Of course, Adrian was right. Rhychard hadn't given her much reason to trust him during that time.

"You never gave her answers, Rhychard. How was she supposed to trust you?"

Rhychard just stared at him. They could argue all day about his relationship with Renny and get nowhere. He didn't have the time to argue with him, however. There were far greater things he needed to discover. "So, the name Vargas means nothing to you?"

The pastor was able to keep his face calm, but his eyes—the eyes always gave you up. "Never heard of it before. Should I have?"

Rhychard glanced around the church property. Two massive buildings and the beginnings of a parking garage covered the grounds that ran from the main road back to a creek that led out to the Indian River. The place was immaculately landscaped with Bahia grass and tall, thin palm trees. Hedges outlined the building on all sides and a children's playground rivaled any that the city could put up. The place had more of a country club feel than a church.

Churches in the twenty-first century had become big business where pastors seemed more like CEOs giving pep rallies instead of preaching sermons. Most had a rock concert vibe as the congregation clapped and waved its hands in a frenzied crescendo right before the big speech. Gone were the days of the small church where honest men and women had calluses on their knees from hours of prayer. There was no serving the community, only number crunching. The church didn't go out to you; they expected you to come to it.

There were dozens of churches just like Harvest Fellowship all across Harbor City, so what made this one so valuable to the Void? Its location was good, but others were better. Obviously, Adrian was just as corruptible as other pastors and there were bigger congregations. It had to be the land itself, but why?

If this property had something worth knowing, I bet a real estate agent would have that knowledge. He needed to talk to Renny. If she would talk to him, that is. He turned his gaze back to Adrian. "No, I suppose you wouldn't." He revved his bike and turned the front wheel back to the main road. "By the way, Buttercup says 'Hello.'"

Pastor Adrian Michaels couldn't hide that facial expression.

Twelve

"Criminals? You want me to believe that Pastor Adrian hangs out with criminals?" It had definitely not gone the way he had hoped. After leaving Adrian standing in the parking lot with his mouth open, Rhychard had gone after Renny, hoping to get some answers to questions he couldn't really ask. The whole secrecy thing of being a Warrior of the Way was a giant obstacle for his fishing expedition for information, but he thought if he substituted criminal for demon she might listen. Of course, as with every conversation between Renny and him since their break up, he guessed wrong. He debated telling her about Buttercup and her role in Adrian's plans, but the way the conversation was going, any mention of him helping a hooker was not going to help his case. "Rhychard, you've been watching too much television. Maybe it's time you got a real job." Renny stood staring at him, arms crossed defiantly across her chest.

He had caught up with her just outside her townhome as she was locking up her car. She tried to hurry into her apartment, but he was able to cut her off, his hands up in surrender. It was enough to get her to stop.

"I have a job," Rhychard said. *It just pays worse than a cops'*. "Renny, look, why do you think I had to keep disappearing on you? There are things happening in this city that people just wouldn't understand. I hear things, like what was going to happen to Captain Relco. I know what I'm talking about here."

"Oh, and you're what, the local superhero? Do you have a cute little costume under your clothes? I know why you kept leaving me, Rhychard. I heard you one night talking to some woman named Tryna. I know what you were too busy doing, and I just bet you were using your little super powers."

Rhychard stood staring, mouth open. "Tryna happens to be more than twice my age. She's helped me more than anyone I know. She's saved my life more times than I can count."

Renny shook her head and tried to walk around him. "And yet, I never heard of her before I heard you talking to her. And just what would your life need saving from, anyway? Go away, Rhychard. I'm tired of your fantasy lifestyle and excuses. I only deal in reality."

He raced to catch up with Renny before she could get to her apartment's main doors. This would go so much easier if he could just tell her the truth, instead of concocting stories he needed her to believe. He couldn't believe she was jealous of Tryna. *The little midget will never let me live that down.* "Fine. Forget criminals and Adrian and all of that. Just tell me what was on that property before Harvest Fellowship bought it. Please." He threw that last word out hoping to appease her but instead it sounded more like begging to him.

Renny turned on him and he had to stop short to keep from getting too far ahead of her. "Why? So you can come up with something to accuse him of?"

So much anger. *Has she really fallen for this guy? He's married for crying out loud!* He took a deep breath, a mixture of surrender and disappointment. *Was that why the gargoyles were swarming over her place? They weren't there to hurt her. They were protecting her for Adrian. Or what if they weren't there for her at all? What if...?* "Was Adrian at your house last night?"

"Rhychard, go away." Renny shoved him aside and continued walking, each step an angry punch.

"Renny, he's married!" Rhychard caught her arm, stopping her. She yanked it from his grasp, but refused to look at him. "I saw you, back at the church, just a little bit ago. You're not that type of girl."

"Not what type of girl, Rhychard?" Her arms were crossed over her chest, her face an angry accusation against whatever he was about to say.

He stared at her for a brief moment, knowing this was his fault. He had sent her into Adrian's arms by not being the man she needed when she needed a man. "You're not the type of girl to keep her love hidden in the shadows. You don't deserve to be anyone's little secret." Rhychard took a deep breath as his eyes dropped to the ground. "Look, I get it. You were hurt and lonely. You went to Adrian for guidance, comfort, and things just...they just happened." He glanced back up into her eyes. "But, Renny, it's wrong. He's married, and a religious leader to boot. How can you sit there every Sunday knowing that you're doing exactly what he's telling his congregation not to do?"

She turned her gaze away from him, but he could see the blush reddening her face as a lone tear snailed down her cheek. She whispered something, but he couldn't make it out. She took a deep breath and then looked up at him. There had been more than one tear.

Rhychard would have been smart to leave it at that, but he always went three sentences too far. "He's the wrong guy for you, Renny. I know you don't believe me, and I wish I could tell you what you need to hear to prove it to you. There are things about him you don't know. He's hurting people and he has to be stopped." The fire of her anger burned up her tears. He knew he had pushed it, knew it even as the words left his mouth, but he couldn't stop talking. *You and your mouth, Rhychard.* It was too late.

"Leave him alone! Adrian wouldn't hurt anyone. He's a good man and you're just stirring up trouble because you're jealous." She slung her purse over her shoulder and for a minute Rhychard thought she was going to hit him with it.

"Yes, I'm jealous, but this isn't about that. I swear. Look, it's your life. You don't have to justify it to me. Just tell me what was on that land. If your pastor is so decent, what will it hurt to tell me, unless you don't believe it was all innocent?"

She stared at him for a moment, the battle of not wanting to tell him and wanting to prove him wrong evident on her face. "Fine. The land was a cemetery for the dregs of life—prisoners, hookers, junkies—people who had no family and had done nothing good with their lives. I helped Ad…Pastor Adrian convince the city to move it and sell the property to Harvest Fellowship. The church even helped with the cost of relocating the graves. Nothing corrupt went on. Nothing evil, at all. What diabolical criminal plot are you going to fabricate with that?"

But the land was soaked in corrupted souls. That had to be it. "Renny, I'm…"

"Go away, Rhychard." Renny Saunders turned and walked away, her steps a mixture of anger and hurt, at him, at herself, at the twists of life.

Rhychard didn't try to stop her this time. Her life was hers as were her delusions. Renny Saunders knew what she was doing and also knew it was wrong. He could only watch her walk away.

Again.

Rhychard slid back onto his bike, his heart a twisted knot of pain. He gripped the handlebars as he stared up into her townhome. He watched the living room light flip on as she crossed in front of the window. She paused, looked down at him, their eyes locking for a heartbeat before she flipped the blinds closed. She was done talking. She had made it quite clear.

He hit the switch that brought the motorcycle roaring to life as he pulled his gaze from the past. Hitting the throttle, he drove away into his future, a future which no longer contained Renny Saunders. He chuckled to himself as he thought of what it did contain—an over-sized mutt, a midget, and a hooker. His life shouldn't have contained any of them. It almost didn't.

When Rhychard had first taken possession of the Guardian Sword, Tryna had vanished, devastated by Jamairlo's death. Word had reached Kendalais that she was returning to her people in the Land Under and had no interest in returning. This apparently was unheard of among the faerie realm. The Seelie were a blindingly loyal people. They followed the Guardian without question, whether they agreed or disagreed with him. Each race in the Land Under had a function and they carried it out without complaint. Actually, they were each quite proud of their purpose, as if doing the bidding of the Guardian was a great honor that could never be refused. Until Tryna, that is. She couldn't take it, anymore, and had resigned her post, a post she had maintained for over three hundred years.

Rhychard thought the timeline skewed. After all, America wasn't even three hundred years old. However, while people may not have inhabited Harbor City, the Unseelie did. According to Kendalais, creatures of the Void ran amuck over the land until humans pressed forward. As the race of man claimed new territory, the Seelie and Unseelie disappeared, pulling back to the safety of their own worlds until they could deal with the humans and their weapons and tools of iron. Eventually, man covered the globe and there was nowhere for the faerie kind to hide. That was when the Unseelie decided to fight back and wipe out mankind.

During all of that time, Tryna aided the Warriors in the region to defeat the demons of the Nether. She helped uncover weaknesses, shared knowledge with the Lore Masters and Bards to ensure the knowledge she acquired was shared with other Keepers. She also fought for more help from the Land Under. As she said, it was their battle. The humans didn't even know a real war was being waged. When Vargas was gathering his forces against the police captain, she knew Jamairlo and Meelim were outmatched. They needed help, but the Warrior Masters refused to send anyone. She tried to get Jamairlo to leave his post, but he refused to abandon the captain, even knowing he would probably die in the process.

As Tryna predicted, he was killed, and she blamed his death and the death of his coshey on the Warrior Masters. She was not going to do it again.

Somehow, it made it back to Tryna that the Guardian had chosen a human to be a Warrior of the Way, one who had no knowledge of the Way or the Void, one who could barely use a butter knife, not to mention a sword. She approached the Seelie Court and begged them to send more Warriors, but again they refused. She knew that if Jamairlo was in over his head, the human would be, as well. She returned to Harbor City, to try and convince Rhychard to stay out of the fight at first, but when he said he was going to see it through, that he had attempted to be rid of the sword and knew it was futile, she stayed to give him the knowledge he needed.

Rhychard felt himself smiling as he banked a right turn. He could still hear Tryna's voice as she threatened Kendalais. "If the Warrior Masters sacrifice Rhychard in this battle, I will go to the Void myself and fight against you with my knowledge. You will protect him as you failed to protect Jamairlo."

Kendalais had stood in his stoic pose for only a moment as he probably debated how serious her threat was. Finally, he simply nodded. "I will do my best."

"You will do better than your best. Your best ended Jamairlo's life."

While Kendalais drilled him with the Guardian Sword, Tryna took him back to school in the lessons of the Way and of a history about which he knew nothing. After they saved John Relco and ruined Vargas's plans, Rhychard had expected the little ellyll to leave once again. So did Kendalais. To their surprise, however, she stayed. She never explained why or made any demands. She was just there whenever Rhychard needed her, which was quite often. She continued to instruct him, sharing her knowledge and the Guardian's expectations. She was one of the few constants in a life that had become a series of variables, and as much as Rhychard hated the direction his life had taken and hated the Seelie for making it that way, he owed Tryna his life and was grateful she had remained a part of it.

His heart tightened as he thought of Renny once again. Tryna had come to his aid when too many others had simply turned their backs. He forced himself to take a deep breath. The past was the past and as much as he wanted it to be his present, he had to worry now about his future; a future without the one he loved most.

Thirteen

Buttercup stood in the kitchen in front of a pan of sizzling bacon. She wore one of his long button-down dress shirts that Rhychard had forgotten he even owned. They obviously hadn't found pants for her because as she stretched to reach for some plates, the shirt rode up her thin legs exposing the bottom curves of her firm ass, the flesh slightly paler than the rest of her body. Rhychard's eyebrows went up as he shifted in his seat, but he didn't look away. He couldn't no matter how much decency said he should. She had showered and finished scraping the remaining makeup off that had plastered her face. The transformation was stunning. Her obsidian hair hung straight and loose down her back in a soft waterfall instead of the hair sprayed curls that had before sat like a crude bird's nest. Her bronze skin was clean and alive now even if a bruise decorated it here and there, and she had gentle eyes with thin soft lips that appeared as if it would hold a natural smile.

:A real flower, isn't she,: Kree's voice echoed in his head.

Rhychard turned and saw the coshey sprawled across his loveseat, his permanent place of residence. *:She cleaned up nice, for sure.:* The Warrior stood as he turned back toward the younger woman who was cooking, walking over and peering into the frying pan. "Bacon?"

"What? Surprised a whore can cook?" Her voice had a bitter edge and her body, soft just a moment ago, went rigid.

"More like I was surprised I had anything edible in here." Rhychard turned and pulled a glass from the cupboard. He then turned on the faucet and filled it with water. "And I don't like that term. Please don't use it again."

Buttercup flipped a slice of bacon in the pan, refusing to look at him. Her body was still tense, but more because of her nerves than anything he had said. "I'm sorry. I'm just…" She shook her head. "I'm used to people thinking that all I can do is lay on my back." She flipped the rest of the bacon as she forced herself to take a deep breath. "You saved my life. I shouldn't be so rude."

Rhychard turned and leaned back against the counter as he sipped the tap water. He nodded as he held the glass in both hands down by his waist. "I'm sure in your profession there isn't a great deal of encouragers. Still, I'll bet you have quite a few skills that could earn you some decent money. Have you ever thought about doing anything else?"

She stared at the greasy pan as the bacon snapped and popped into its delicious state of sustenance. He didn't push her, allowing her the space that she probably wasn't used to. Finally she just shrugged. "I wanted to be a teacher at one point. Help kids not turn into me."

Rhychard laid a hand on her shoulder, making her turn and look at him. He could feel the hardness of her bones with no flab to soften her up. "There is nothing wrong with you except some negative thinking. You'd probably make a great teacher. You just need to go for it." He gave a soft squeeze and set his glass on the counter. "I mean, hey, I thought I was only a moving man. Now look at me."

Buttercup smiled, her lips thin over her white teeth. "Go wash up. Food is almost ready."

He smiled as he pushed away from the counter to the meager area he called a living room. *:Tryna here?:* He sent to Kree as he entered the tiny hall.

:In the bedroom.:

Rhychard turned right and went to find the faerie. When he opened the bedroom door, he found her standing in front of his window staring out at the forest beyond. Her head barely cleared the window sill as she stood with her hands clasped behind her back, her tiny sandaled feet peeking out from under her long burgundy dress.

"I think I know what Vargas wants with the church," he said as he joined her by the window. He sat on the window sill so that he would be closer to being eye to eye with her. It didn't help much, but it was a nice attempt. "Harvest Fellowship sits on what used to be a cemetery for undesirables. I'm sure the ground is soaked in the life energy of hundreds of people swallowed by the Void. I'd wager that's why he wants it, but for what reason, I'm not sure."

Tryna stared out the window, her long blond hair draped over her thin shoulders. Her small body was tense as she stood there. "How do you think I get here, Rhychard?"

He shrugged. "You pop in and out, usually at inopportune times. I never really thought about it. Why?"

She turned as she faced him, her face showing her disappointment. "I have really failed in your training, I see." Her voice held tiredness to it as she scolded—him or her? She leaned back against the window sill, which came to her shoulders. "Ah, well, no time but the present, I suppose. When I pop in or out, as you call it, I'm merely going from, say, here to the park. Still, it's in this world. However, where I come from is another place altogether, another dimension, the Land Under you call it. You couldn't pronounce the elven name. It's the dimension where all the faerie creatures live, elves, dwarves, gnomes, coshey, and others. We've lived there for eons, protected from the Void while we strive to rid your world of its influence. Creatures of the Void live in the Nether, a desolate wasteland where demons and trolls, giants and ogres, and all creatures of vile origin strive to destroy your world, so that they may get to ours. The battle between the Way and the Void has raged for millions of years and earth has been the battlefield for most of it.

"A Gateway has to be opened in order for any of the peoples of faerie to cross from the Land Under to this world. It takes great power on soil cultivated by the Seelie for a portal to be opened. The same is true of Gateways to the Nether only in reverse. The Void requires ground it can twist and which has seen a lot of evil."

A Gateway to the Nether, now that would be a living nightmare. "Wait. Don't they have a Gateway here now? I mean, they're here so they have to have a way to get here. Why would they want another?"

She shook her head. "They travel, as do I. There is not another Gateway for a hundred miles for either the Land Under or the Nether. The Destroyer would have a sizable advantage over this region if he could open one for his people."

Rhychard had a hard time thinking of demons and gargoyles as people. Still, it didn't make sense to him. "But Harvest Fellowship is Sacred Ground."

"It wasn't originally and if what you discovered is correct it looks like it won't be much longer. Perhaps that's what Vargas wants it for. Depending on how long the cemetery has been there it could be soaked in negative energy, and if Mr. Michaels is turning his congregation from the path of the Way, it could be all Vargas needs to use the land for his purposes."

Rhychard glanced back out at the trees behind his house, oaks and elders with a couple of towering pines thrown in. It was an oasis for him. He could walk into those woods and the noise of life faded the deeper he went, the churning waters of the river calling him, soothing him. He wanted to walk in them now and forget Vargas and Adrian, Harvest Fellowship and cemeteries. He wanted to forget Renny.

He felt Tryna's tiny hand on his arm and glanced down at her. "Rhychard, to open a Gateway to the Void takes blood, lots of blood."

"And Harvest Fellowship has about four hundred in their congregation on any given Sunday. That's a lot of blood." *What is it with demons and blood? Why can't they just once perform a simple ritual with a dance and a chant and then go for an espresso?*

Tryna returned her gaze to the woods as she turned back around. Dusk was starting to cast its lengthy shadows over the earth. "I need to go see someone. I need to see if I can find some answers. We have to be able to turn the tide, and I am at a loss as to how right now. This is knowledge I do not have."

Rhychard nodded. If Tryna didn't know how to defeat Vargas, he wasn't sure who would.

There was a soft knock on the door. Buttercup pushed it open a bare crack. "Dinner is ready." She didn't wait for an answer, but instead turned and walked back to the kitchen.

Rhychard stared at the door. It had been a long time since someone had cooked for him. Renny had been the last, actually. "How does a church stop being Sacred Ground?" He asked on his way to the door, stopping when he got there to turn and face Tryna.

"As the leader goes, so go the people. Enough compromise and soon the Way is lost."

Cavorting with demons and adultery. Yea, I'd say our good pastor has compromised. "How long will you be gone?"

"As long as it takes, but, hopefully, not longer than is needed."

Rhychard nodded and then followed the path Buttercup made to the kitchen. Vargas was going to kill Adrian Michaels and the congregation to open his Gateway, and the pastor probably didn't even realize that his life was part of whatever deal he had made with the demon. Renny was a part of that congregation. *This sucks. In order to save the girl I love that no longer loves me, I have to save the man she's having an affair with, the man I'd rather beat the shit out of.*

The smell of bacon filled the air in his small apartment. Kree was already scarfing down enough crispy pig to cause a middle-aged man a heart attack and Tryna had popped out by the sound of tinkling bells that came from the bedroom. Buttercup set a plate on the table with what looked like a BLT sandwich without the T and very wilted L. Some crumbs left from an ancient potato chip bag were piled beside it.

"You don't exactly have much in the way of food here," Buttercup said as she sat in a chair across from him. She had Cheetos on her plate, or the remnants of what was once Cheetos. *Where did those come from?* "How do you eat?" She tasted the faded orange snack as if unsure of its safety.

:Rhychard's on a first name basis with the Domino's Pizza delivery man,: Kree mind-spoke.

Rhychard felt his face blush and had no idea why he was suddenly embarrassed. "I don't see any reason to keep a lot of food around. It usually goes bad before I'm able to eat it. Besides, demons and telemarketers have one thing in common; they both call during dinner."

"I'm surprised you have the strength to fight them the way you eat," Buttercup said as she took a bite of her sandwich, pinkies extended outward.

Rhychard glanced down at the measly meal. *I guess I* should *eat better. I'm going to need my strength as it looks like Rhychard Bartlett is going to church to fight demons.* He didn't relish the idea even if it was to thwart the bad guys. When Renny and he had split, those that he had called friends suddenly wanted nothing to do with him. People pretended not to see him when they were out or started ignoring his calls. Eventually, he had just stopped going to church and the sad part was no one seemed to miss him.

Buttercup wiped her hands on a semi-dirty towel, went to wipe her mouth with it and then thought better of it. "So, how did you wind up doing what it is you do?"

Rhychard scooped the potato chip crumbs into his fingers and sprinkled them into his mouth, the crumbs wanting to stick to his skin. He sipped the water Buttercup had poured him as there was nothing else to drink in the place. He really needed to get to the store. He told Buttercup about how he had come across Jamairlo and fighting the gargoyles, how the elf had given him the Guardian Sword just before dying, promising someone would come for it. He saw no sense in hiding it from her since she was in the middle of it anyway. The truth was it felt good to finally talk about it to someone besides Kree and Tryna. "What Jamairlo left out was the part where they weren't coming for the sword, but for me. A couple of days later Kendalais, another elf, showed up telling me that the Guardian had chosen a pitiful human to be a Warrior of the Way."

"Pitiful human?" Buttercup had both hands around her glass, her eyes intent on Rhychard.

"Yeah, elves have a snobbish sense of superiority about them. They think they are far better than the human race."

:Every race, for that matter.: Kree sat on his haunches by the table but his head was almost even with theirs. *:They are the oldest race, born of the gods, and humans the youngest, so the elves see humans as children who like playing Grown Up.:*

Buttercup shook her head. "So if they thought they could do better, why didn't they just take the sword back?"

Rhychard spun his drink in slow circles on the table, his eyes watching the light reflect off the clear glass. "Trust me, I wish it would have been that simple. However, once the Guardian chooses you, your course is set and nothing can change that, not even you. I know, I tried, but once chosen there resides this…this…" He waved his hands trying to think of the right way to say it. "It's like this burning inside you that you can't ignore. The sword calls you until, before you go crazy, you snatch it up and go do what it wants you to do. You can't even throw the blasted thing away." He knew because he had tried and it almost killed him.

"That would suck." Buttercup leaned back in her chair.

Kendalais had spent quite a bit of time describing the power of the sword. It was the one weapon the Guardian had made in the beginning. He was a god of creation, not destruction. Yet, he had made one for every Warrior he planned on calling and imbued it with the power to detect the Unseelie with a blue glow and radiating heat. Iron is deadly to the faerie, so the Guardian made the swords out of bronze and empowered them with a magic that would not only detect the Unseelie, but destroy them, as well. He also gave it the power to remember. The Guardian Swords were passed from Warrior to Warrior as each passed and another was called. The soul of the dead Warrior was somehow held within the sword. The Guardian knew when a Warrior was about to die and called the next, so that they would be there to retrieve the sword. It was not permitted to fall into the hands of the Unseelie for they would turn one over to the Destroyer who would then convert it and turn its power against the Seelie. When it was Jamairlo's time to die, there were no other elves in the area because of the Warrior Masters' stubbornness. The Guardian chose Rhychard. The sword retains the memories and skills of each Warrior that used the blade along with their soul, enabling the current Warrior to draw upon their experiences in battle, gaining strength as he fought. That power had changed Rhychard in subtle ways, making him stronger, thicker. It had also ruined his life.

Rhychard stood and started collecting the plates. Kree padded over to the sofa and reclaimed his spot while Buttercup helped gather the dishes. As he turned the faucet on he said, "Kendalais helped me learn how to use the sword, explaining the glamour that makes it disappear until I touch it. A glamour is a spell that alters the appearance of something. That's how the elves move among us; they can make themselves seem human." He started washing the plates while she dried and put them away. "Too bad they can't act human," he said.

"Anyway, while Kendalais was teaching me how not to get killed, Tryna taught me about the battle between the Way and the Void." He shrugged as he handed her a glass. "I'm not a very good student, which is why she is still here."

Buttercup nodded behind her at the elven hound on the couch. "And your friend over there?"

:I came along to keep Tryna from killing him.: Kree's smile could be heard in his voice.

Rhychard gave her a sheepish smile. "As I said, I'm not the best student."

Once the dishes were done, which in itself was a new experience for Rhychard, he grabbed a cigar and a beer and perched himself on the railing of his back porch where he could stare out at the forest. He had left the sliding door open so that Buttercup would feel welcome to join him if she was so inclined. He wondered how Tryna was doing and who she was going to see. More than likely she ventured to the Land Under. Somehow they had to stop Vargas, and Rhychard knew that he was still too new to the game to figure it out on his own.

Buttercup joined him on the back porch after pouring herself some more water. She eased herself into the empty camp chair as she took in the surroundings. "You have a peaceful view."

Rhychard nodded as he took a pull from his cigar. "It helps to look at it and remind myself of the beauty in the world."

She didn't say anything, just nodded.

He turned and took her in. She was still too scrawny and reminded him of those starving kids from Third World countries that they exploited on television to get people to send money. Her eyes still had that sunken look to them, but otherwise she was beautiful. How did she get caught up in the streets?

:Just because someone is pretty doesn't mean they have it made.: Kree chided him. *:Sometimes life forces people into tough decisions and down paths they never had planned. I'm sure you can attest to that, Warrior.:*

Rhychard turned back to the trees that blocked his view of the creek. He could understand completely. One time at playing Good Samaritan had changed his life completely. Furthermore, because his life had changed, Renny's had changed, and now she was on the wrong path. Her pain had driven her into the arms of a married man. He wondered if Adrian loved her in return or if it was just a casual fling for the pastor.

"How could that pastor hurt those people?" Buttercup was staring at her glass as she spoke. "He's supposed to be leading them into Heaven, right? I mean, they trusted him."

Rhychard wished he had a straight forward answer for her, but as Kree had said, who knows what life hands people that pushes them in their choices. That was all he could tell her. He simply didn't know why people did half of what they did. Although, with Adrian he figured it had to be a lust for power. The pastor wouldn't have been the first religious leader to mistake his inner greed for God's voice. Once a person starts down that road it is easy to rationalize each decision thereafter. Eventually, a person would find themselves going in the complete opposite direction of where they had been heading and not even remember how they got there.

Rhychard glanced back at Buttercup and wondered if that had been her story. What decision had she been forced to make that led her to the streets of Harbor City? Whatever it was, it hadn't been enough to sway her completely. She still had a conscience or else she wouldn't be sitting with him now. Perhaps that meant there was still hope for Renny. Perhaps he could still save her. Perhaps Buttercup proved that it was never too late to turn your life back around.

He closed his eyes tight, the anguish of his heart filling him. Perhaps.

Fourteen

Every Monday night Harvest Fellowship's deacons gathered in the pastor's conference room, twenty men selected by the congregation that best represented Christian values to assist Pastor Adrian Michaels in carrying out the ministry of the church. Rhychard knew most of those men, had hung out with them, had dinner with them. He had even worked alongside them in several ministry projects. Of course, that was before Renny had accused him of cheating on her and dumped him. Now no one at Harvest Fellowship would even say hello to him.

Miles Evans had been an exception. The man loved gossip and didn't care where he got it. Rhychard had known that about the man since he met him. He was also given to off-colored jokes that were borderline crude, which had surprised Rhychard considering Miles was a leader in the church. Of course, it was now quite obvious that something was rotten at Harvest Fellowship, and that standards were to be preached, not followed.

Men started slipping out of the glass door on the side of Harvest Fellowship, making their way to the cars in the litter-free parking lot. Miles walked out; a stack of notebooks tucked under one arm as he slapped the youth pastor on the back, the two men laughing about something. The Head Usher walked off to a burnt orange PT Cruiser, slid in and drove off. Rhychard watched the obnoxious man pull away. He didn't want to talk to him. Ever again, if he could help it.

David Morsetti slumped out of the church alone. His hands were stuffed into his pockets and his balding head bent toward the ground before him. He wasn't laughing with the others. He wasn't even talking to the others. He stayed to himself and trudged his way over to his small red Jeep. Whereas Miles bounced into his vehicle, David surrendered. The other deacons and pastors seemed lighthearted and untroubled, so whatever had David weighted down, it didn't happen in the meeting.

David drove the same as he walked, sluggish. He seemed in no hurry to go home and wasn't even hitting the speed limit. Rhychard swung his bike behind the Jeep and fought his impatience to pass. He needed to talk to David. He had always liked the Sunday school teacher. Renny and he had sat in on the man's class even though they weren't married. He taught couples to be stronger, to overcome the struggles and temptations of life. Yet, somehow, he had managed to be alone with Buttercup. She said he had spent the car ride trying to convince her to leave life on the streets. He had even offered to help her. Yet, according to his teaching, he shouldn't have been alone with her in the car to begin with. The first time he had slipped had trapped him and made him a pawn of Adrian's.

David turned south on Washington Street and headed downtown. *Not going home, David?* Rhychard followed a few car lengths behind, curiosity making him cautious. He could just make out the swivel of the other man's head as he scanned parking lots, back alleys, and side streets. His speed had dropped to a crawl as his search controlled him. At first, Rhychard thought David was looking for a girl on the streets to hook up with, but after he drove past three willing transactions it dawned on Rhychard that David's search was specific.

He was looking for Buttercup.

David took two passes up and down the working girl's strip, his concentration on finding the girl he thought set him up so strong that he didn't notice the crotch rocket keeping pace with him. At the third pass, he gave up and pulled into Saunders' Realty's parking lot, his headlights skimming the calm river waters. Rhychard slowed and watched as his former teacher climbed out of the vehicle and walked around to the front to lean back on the grill. His hands were back in his pockets, shoulders slumped. *Why is he looking for Buttercup?*

Rhychard swung into the parking lot, pulling next to the faded Jeep. If David heard him he gave no sign. The breeze pulled at Rhychard's hair, which he had forgotten to tie back. He made a mental feel for the Guardian Sword, but it was cold. No evil creatures about. Of course, that didn't mean the human variety wasn't around. As he swung off the bike, he noticed David didn't even turn his head. He kept his eyes on the slow moving water of the Indian River, his mind obviously in some far off place.

"She's not here." Rhychard slipped his hands into his coat pockets, trying to look casual.

David turned his head, noticed Rhychard, and turned back around with a nod. "I'm not here to see Renny. I just needed a quiet place to think." He turned his gaze back to Rhychard, his chocolate eyes lost in some inner turmoil. "Are you two back together? Good. You both made a great couple." He faced the water again. "I'm glad she forgave you."

Rhychard shook his head as he stepped in front of David, forcing the man to look at him. "Renny and I are still a broken issue, but I wasn't referring to her. I meant Buttercup isn't on the streets. Isn't she who you were looking for?"

David's eyes went wide and Rhychard saw that panicked look that tensed the man's entire body. Rhychard slipped his right hand out of his pocket in case David lashed out, but the man just slumped in on himself, deflated. "What's done in secret will be shouted from the rooftops." He ran a thick hand over his bald scalp and down across the ringlet of dark hair he had left as he took a deep breath. "So it begins."

"What, David? What begins?"

"Rhychard, I didn't do anything." His eyes looked as if they pleaded for Rhychard to believe the words spoken. "I don't care what Pastor Adrian says. I did not have sex with that girl."

Rhychard knew he hadn't. "You were made to look as if you had, but she was still in your Jeep."

Defeat turned to angry desperation faster than Rhychard could take a breath and David lunged at the Warrior, knocking him to the ground. "You son of a bitch! It was you. You set me up." A fist caught Rhychard's brow, another connected with his ribs. "Why? What did I ever do to you?"

So much for Christians being meek. David was a thick mass of swinging arms and thrashing legs as he tried to straddle Rhychard's waist. He kept lashing out, connecting wherever he could. It took several blows before Rhychard could twist his hips enough to toss the heavier man off him. He used the excess of his jacket to slow the swinging fists from pummeling him into one giant bruise. Rhychard didn't try to defend the accusations, just his body. He rolled on top of the squirming man and caught each of his fists. Once both fleshly weapons were caught, he pinned them to David's chest and pressed down. His ribs screamed as the angry deacon kicked and twisted under him trying to get free.

"David! David, knock it off! I didn't do it." The man wasn't listening. Rhychard needed to become a better observer of body language. "David, don't make me hurt you! I didn't set you up. I was here talking to Renny when I saw Buttercup get out of your car. I didn't know what was going on at the time. I do now."

David stopped struggling, his chest lifting Rhychard slightly with heavy breaths. "Get off."

"Are you going to hit me again?"

David just shook his head. Rhychard eased his grip a little. When David made no move to attack again, he released the man and stood up. He extended an arm, offering David a hand up. The defeated look was back in his eyes as he took the offered hand and allowed himself to be pulled to his feet. He brushed himself off as Rhychard stood, poised for another outburst.

With a deep breath, David stood straight and apologized. "I just assumed since you knew about it that you were in on it. I don't know what to believe anymore or who to trust."

"I know the feeling." Rhychard shook his coat out as he walked back to the Jeep. If David was still being followed by the anonymous photographer, their little fight would have given him a great photo opportunity. "But, David, I promise you can trust me."

David stared back at the water. A couple of pelicans floated on the surface, their bodies dipping like buoys with the tiny waves. Rhychard could see the inner struggle going on within him. The man was scared. He should be. If what Buttercup had told them was going on was actually happening, then David was on the verge of having his life ruined. "You can't fight this alone."

David turned and faced him, hands on hips. "How do you even know what *this* is? If you're not in on it, how do you know who Buttercup is? You want me to trust you, but you already seem way ahead of me."

"Okay. Fair questions. I did see you drop Buttercup off the other day, but I didn't know who she was at the time, only what she did. The next day I rescued her from an attack set up by your pastor because she grew a conscience. I know what Adrian is doing, David. I'm just not sure why."

David shrugged. "He needs my votes on some things that I was against. If I vote his way, then my wife doesn't see the pictures."

"If you didn't do anything, what are the pictures of?"

"She got in the car, got out of the car." He glanced up at the crescent moon, his body tense. "While she was in the car she bent over to grab a lipstick container she had dropped. The picture makes it look like…it looks like she's performing oral sex, Rhychard, but I swear nothing happened."

Rhychard reached a hand out and gripped the other man's upper arm. "Relax, David. I already know nothing happened. Buttercup told me everything. It's actually because you didn't try to have sex with her that made her regret what she was doing. You weren't the only person set up, but you were one of the few that didn't take her up on her offer. She knew what was going to happen and it disgusted her. You didn't deserve the cruelty that was about to rain down on you."

"Others?"

Rhychard filled him in on what Buttercup had told them and how Adrian Michaels had several people in varying positions throughout the city. He was making Harvest Fellowship an empire and he wasn't waiting on God's timing or provisions. It was easy to make him believe Adrian was just a greedy corrupt religious leader. Rhychard decided it best, however, to leave Vargas out of the explanation. David Morsetti had enough to think about.

"When my wife sees those pictures…" David just stared off again. His voice was shaky and Rhychard could actually see the tightness in the man's chest.

"She won't. I'll keep that from happening," Rhychard said. "Where does Adrian keep them?"

David walked away from the Jeep and into the grass that led to the drop to the rocks bordering the Indian River. He stared down into the water as it lapped at the algae-covered rocks. "He showed me the pictures in his office. I guess he keeps them there. It's like a vault in there, so it's safe." His hands were buried in his pockets and Rhychard knew that the man wasn't seeing the water he was staring at. "I knew better. I've taught that married men shouldn't be alone with another woman, and yet, I made the choice to stop." He shook his head. "I'm not going to hide this from my wife. Trying to hide it will only make it worse."

Rhychard walked up behind David and put his hand on his shoulders. "You are a good man, David, and I will talk to Sylvia if you need me to, but I need to stop Adrian."

"Why, Rhychard?" David turned to him, his voice stressed and confused. "What does any of this have to do with you?"

Rhychard couldn't tell him the truth. He would probably believe him that Adrian was having an affair with Renny. He wouldn't, however, believe Rhychard about demons and gargoyles. Hell, he had been fighting for three months as a Warrior of the Way and he still didn't believe it. "All I can say is there is more going on than you know."

David just nodded. Rhychard gave the man's shoulder a reassuring squeeze. "Go home, David. I'll take care of this."

"I will in a minute. I just need to be alone a bit."

Rhychard told him not to be away from his wife too long. He then slipped into the saddle of his Suzuki and headed to the condo. Hopefully, Kree was being lazy on his couch. Rhychard needed a lookout and one with mind-speech was a bonus. There was plenty of night left and knowing the lax security of Harvest Fellowship, the alarm codes would still be the same even a few months and missing members later. Rhychard was going inside that church, one way or another.

Fifteen

:Are you sure this is a proper plan?:

"As long as the alarm doesn't get tripped, what can go wrong?"

:That's usually the last sentence before chaos rains down upon us. Did you not say the same thing at that warehouse with John Relco?:

Rhychard ignored the giant coshey and focused instead on the deadbolt he was trying to convince to let him in. Kree had been sound asleep when Rhychard arrived at his small condo. It had taken a little convincing to get the giant mutt to agree to stand guard, but in the end it worked out. Kree was perched on the gray-shingled roof, his gaze scanning for intruders, while Rhychard was trying to recall what the Internet had shown him about picking a lock.

The plan was simple. Once Rhychard managed to get inside Adrian's office, he would search for the pictures that Buttercup had helped arrange. If he could get his hands on those, then the good pastor would lose his leverage. The men could stop following his orders and, with the proof turned over to David Morsetti, Adrian would be dismissed as pastor and Vargas's plan for the little church to be used as a Gateway would be thwarted. He would have saved the day as a Warrior was supposed to and all without drawing the Guardian Sword.

The evening was cool with a slight breeze rustling the palm trees. He knew the place was empty. Churches didn't really beef up their security system. There were no cameras or extra alarms on individual offices. They were also pretty free with keys and passing out the alarm code, which never made sense to Rhychard. Why worry about securing the building at all if every schmoe was going to have access to the place?

The lock clicked. Rhychard jerked the door open to the beep beep of the alarm counting down the thirty seconds before a screeching wail would announce the intruder and the police would be notified. He had been given the code a year ago when he had volunteered Trace and he to go in and help move some offices around. He punched in the four digit code and the beeping ceased.

:I'm in. How does it look out there?:

:Dark.:

Rhychard made his way down the hall toward Adrian's office. *:I'm glad sunrise didn't come early.: Smart ass.*

:I heard that.:

:That's totally unfair. Stay out of my head.:

:But there is so much free space to roam.:

Rhychard picked the door that led to the string of offices, choosing to ignore the elven hound's remark. The emergency lighting cast an eerie glow over the neat desks and file cabinets. The office area of Harvest Fellowship began with a receptionist's desk to weed out those that would steal too much time from one of the overloaded pastors. A doorway opened up to three other desks which were used by secretaries that were shared among the four pastors. After them began the hallway leading to the secluded pastors who were locked away from the rest of the congregation.

The first three doors he passed led to the offices of the assisting pastors, each with a specific job description. They were sort of like assistant managers assigned different departments in a retail store. James Henderson served as music minister, Russell Hendrickson was the youth pastor, and Bryan Lawson was the education minister. Rhychard had liked each one and each seemed like a faithful leader, but he wondered now how many of them had fallen off the straight and narrow.

Rhychard picked his way into Adrian's office, closing the door behind him. He stood inside the largest of the pastoral offices and took it all in. Two windows faced east, their white blinds closed and free of dust. In front of the windows were two burgundy high-backed chairs with a table and lamp between them. As Rhychard looked around, he noticed that the whole place was dust free. Immaculate. Four oak bookshelves lined the south wall filled with resource books and commentaries, devotionals and biographies. In front of the shelves rested Adrian's wide desk where every folder and knickknack was perfectly in its proper place. There was a picture of Diane Michaels and their three girls, each named after a major Biblical character. Awards and diplomas decorated the walls and two burgundy chairs sat in front of the desk just waiting for a counseling session to begin. Along the north wall was a closet with bi-fold doors. The entrance to the office had been on the west wall.

Rhychard tried the closet first. Even it was immaculate. *Who keeps their closet organized?*

:Not everyone is a massive slob.:

The Warrior continued to ignore the coshey. The closet was for storage, not clothes, so it had shelves stacked with counseling materials, Gospel tracts and excess books. Rhychard picked up a small paperback. *What to Expect from Your Spouse*. He held it tight as his chest felt a painful constriction. Renny and he would have had to read the book. They would have if things had turned out differently, that is. He wondered how Pastor Adrian could teach from such a book knowing he was doing the exact opposite. The man was cheating on his wife while telling others to remain faithful.

:He would not be the first religious hypocrite to do so.: Kree spoke in the Warrior's mind. *:Why do you think Adrian would keep his blackmail material here?:*

:He would want it close in order to prove to his victims he had it. He can't exactly have these meetings at home.:

There was nothing in the closet. He had even looked for secret panels like he had seen in all of those spy movies. The closet was just a closet. Rhychard moved to the desk and continued the search. Just like the closet, everything was neat and tidy and in its proper place. There were organizers for pens, paperclips, and rubber bands. His files were crisp and had computerized labels giving them an orderly appearance. Not one piece of paper had a coffee stain or wrinkle. How did he manage to get any work done in such a sterile environment?

The drawers were a dead end. Rhychard felt around edges and behind drawers, inside each little whatnot and behind every picture. Nothing. He sat in one of the leather chairs, his back to the window, as he stared at the office.

:How goes it, Warrior?:

:Either Harvest Fellowship has the best custodian in the world or our good pastor is a little OCD. Nothing is out of place.: Rhychard scanned the walls, the desk, the bookshelves…the books? Rhychard stood and scanned the books on the shelf. They were alphabetized within subjects. Prayer. Commentaries. Biographies. Between a Biblical concordance and a topical Bible was a large hardbound book on American Baseball. "Now, you're out of place, aren't you?" He slipped the book from its place and was surprised at how light it was compared to its notebook size. *:I think I found something.:*

:I was afraid you had fallen asleep.:

It was a hollow box, one of those storage boxes that you could buy in a craft store that at first glance seemed like a real book, but was truly a hiding place for secrets. In this case, it had a ton of photos of men in compromising positions with Buttercup. Rhychard felt his face flush as he glanced through them. There were also a couple of small SD cards that probably held the digital versions of the blackmail photos. Rhychard scooped everything out of the fake tome and slid it back in its place.

As he turned around, ready to make good his escape, chaos erupted around him. Kree screamed out as the Guardian Sword pulsed a blue heat along his back. Glass exploded, slicing Rhychard in small tiny cuts as sharp talons dug into his shoulders knocking him up and onto the desk. He could feel every small object on Adrian's desk as it dug into his back, the letter opener embedding itself in his shoulder. The pictures in his hand went flying everywhere.

Rhychard rolled the rest of the way off the desk as he heard the gargoyle slam into the opposite wall. As he hurled to his feet, he reached over his shoulder and gripped the hilt of the Guardian Sword. The warmth of the blade's magic filled him and he could sense the power filling him as well as the voices of long dead Warriors. He tried to ignore them as he held the blade in front of him, its steel a bright blue that lit the room in an eerie glow outshining the emergency lights in the hallway

The gargoyle turned, its wings close to its leathery body as it reached his claws out trying to grab Rhychard. The Warrior jumped backward and out of reach. The beast lunged, but its thighs caught the desk, bringing it to a quick halt. As it fell forward it swiped at Rhychard's coat. The Warrior jerked back, slashing across with his sword. The blade sliced into the gargoyle's shoulder, continuing deep into its chest. The creature screamed before bursting into a cloud of ash.

:Kree!:

:Get out, Warrior! Two more are approaching.:

He climbed out the shattered window, broken glass trickled to the ground below. He forced his way over the shrubs that bordered the church, the Guardian Sword poised in front of him. *:Where?:* They must have the church staked out, but why wait so long to strike? Rhychard stepped away from the bushes while keeping his back to the building.

:East.:

Rhychard could hear Kree's claws scraping against the shingles above him. The elven hound was running. Rhychard faced east and waited. Two dots moved in the darkness, barely perceived in the moonlight. He braced as the dots took shape and became gargoyles. :*Is this it? It seems kind of small for a protective detail.*:

Sirens cracked the silence as red and blue lights spun off the buildings and trees that lined Hudson Avenue. Rhychard watched as they drew closer. He knew he had turned off the alarm. There was no way they could have known that Rhychard was there. He tightened his grip on the Guardian Sword as he turned back to the gargoyles.

But they weren't moving. They just hovered in place. Waiting.

:*Warrior, glance behind the gargoyles, along the tree line.*:

Rhychard followed the tree line until he spotted the demon. Vargas stood, hands clasped behind him, and watched. Even in the dark and across the flat field, Rhychard could see the creature's grin.

The sirens screamed as the cop cars came into sight. :*We have to get out of here.*: The gargoyles weren't sent to attack him, just to keep him busy until the police arrived. Rhychard turned back to the shattered window. The police cars, two of them, squealed into the parking lot. There was no time to go back for the pictures.

He heard the heavy thud of the coshey as Kree landed beside him. :*To the creek, Warrior. Now!*:

Rhychard didn't question. He simply turned and ran to the oaks and pines that separated Harvest Fellowship from Pelican Creek. The gargoyles screeched and began to chase. From the distance, Rhychard could hear the demon's cackle.

He should have known that something such as those pictures would be guarded by more than electronics. Vargas still couldn't come all the way onto Sacred Ground and the gargoyles never touched down. The balance between the Way and the Void must have shifted enough to allow the first flying bat to bust through the office window. Things were getting worse.

As soon as they entered the trees, Rhychard turned to see if they were being followed. The police had parked by the entrance and the broken window. Guns were drawn, but their attention was on the building, not the woods. "They didn't see us."

:*But they did.*: Rhychard could feel Kree's mental finger point to the east.

The gargoyles folded their leather wings against their sinewy bodies and zipped through the branches heading to Rhychard. :*Move back to the creek.*: Rhychard turned and moved deeper into the trees. :*The police can't hear us there.*: If they drew too much attention, the police would find them.

He had expected to be killed like Jamairlo when he had been forced into service of the Guardian. Not arrested. Rhychard bet this had never happened to other Warriors.

He found a small clearing that had several intertwining branches overhead providing a low ceiling. The gargoyles would not be able to attack from above. It was a smart place to take a stand.

:The religious leader is here.:

Rhychard turned and faced the north, the snapping branches warning him of the gargoyles' approach. *:How do you know that?:* He spread his feet shoulder-width apart as he held the Guardian Sword with both hands. Warmth tinged his fingers as the cold steel took on a bluish hue.

Kree stood behind him, his tail wagging back and forth like a cat ready to pounce. *:I am a coshey. We have excellent hearing and smell. His arrogance can be heard for miles. And he stinks.:*

A branch snapped and the first gargoyle plunged into the clearing followed immediately by the second. Kree turned and leaped into the air, paws extended. Rhychard ducked to his right and slashed at the second creature. The gargoyle braced his wings trying to halt his momentum. He wasn't fast enough. The Guardian Sword sliced through the beast's chest, ripping it open. It screeched slicing the air with its dying wail before exploding into ash. So much for not drawing attention to them.

Rhychard turned to aid Kree. The elven hound and gargoyle were wrapped around each other in a wrestling match on the ground. Kree yelped as a claw ripped his chest, then he bit into one of the wings with his massive jaws and ripped. The gargoyle screamed, stretching his head back as he wailed his pain at the moon. Rhychard brought his sword down across the beast's outstretched neck, ending the wail. Kree fell to the earth and sneezed. *:I hate the way they die.:*

"I agree, but better that than having to explain a gargoyle corpse." Rhychard strained to hear, but the sirens had been shut off, leaving only the spinning lights. The Guardian Sword still held its blue glow. "We're not alone, yet."

Kree stood to his feet, his hackles raised as he turned to the east. A low growl rolled from his belly.

Rhychard turned, sword raised, and watched as Vargas stepped around a giant oak. He clapped his grayish hand-like claws as he bowed slightly. His blue-gray hair hung about his neck and shoulders like a waterfall. "It was a nice attempt, Rhychard. I always learn so much from watching you."

Vargas's voice was like silk, soft and gentle. "You helped me see Adrian's weakness. You are like one of those security consultants."

"My pleasure," Rhychard said, the point of the sword aimed at Vargas's chest, which just so happened to be even with the Warrior's nose. "As your consultant allow me to advise you to go to Hell."

The demon chuckled. "No such place, Rhychard, and by now you know that. Besides, I like this church. It has such beautiful surroundings."

Rhychard just stared. Vargas was smart, too smart to trap into revealing more of his plan. Besides, what else did he need to know? The Unseelie wanted the property to open a Gateway to the Nether.

Vargas's eyes narrowed into slits, his catlike red eyes tiny pinpricks. "This is not your battle, human. Why do you fight for the Seelie? Have they not stolen enough of your life that you will sacrifice the rest for them?"

"If I've understood things correctly, the Unseelie wish to destroy my world in order to gain access to the Land Under. I think that makes this my battle. Besides, I don't like you."

:Warrior, those law enforcement officials are beginning to search in this direction.:

Vargas was trying to stall him. Rhychard kept the sword between the demon and himself as he started to move to the creek. Kree followed behind, his head swinging back and forth for scents of danger, his ears perked, listening. Vargas watched them leave without trying to stop them. His smile had returned.

"I have never done you harm, Rhychard. Not directly. The Seelie will use you as their pawn. You believe them without even hearing the other side. How do you know it is not they who are lying?" The demon began to back away as sounds of the searching officers filtered down to where they stood. Beams of light bounced off trees and shrubs as flashlights were used to sweep the area. "You trust too easily, Rhychard." The demon turned and disappeared, vanishing before he had finished his turn.

Rhychard stared at the empty spot for only a moment before turning and following Kree through the woods and down to the creek. Once they reached Pelican Creek they turned west heading in the opposite direction of the demon. Vargas's words echoed in Rhychard's mind as they paced the creek bank until he had reached his motorcycle. As much as he hated to admit it, the Unseelie demon was correct. Rhychard had just swallowed everything Tryna and Kendalais had spoon fed him. How did he know any of what they said was true? He had taken everything on faith with the rush of adrenaline and events. What if he was being played?

:Warrior, I hear your struggle. Vargas is manipulating your thoughts. He wants to distract you with doubt.:

Rhychard swung a leg over his seat and sat. "I've been manipulated since Jamairlo handed me this damn sword. I'm forced into a war I didn't want and it wasn't the Unseelie who drafted me." He pushed the switch and the Suzuki roared to life. "There is no history, Kree, for me to prove your words true or false. Hell, most people would want me locked away if this ever came to light."

:You have seen the Void. You fought them to defend Captain John Relco. How can you still doubt?:

Rhychard gripped the handlebars. Kree had stayed out of sight, making his way back home on his own. "The same way people doubt when a five-year-old dies of cancer even though they've seen the birth." With a push of his heel, he slipped the kickstand in place and drove off. Vargas had been right about one thing. Rhychard was a pawn in this war.

Sixteen

"I know you're in there!" Anger. A male voice. A fist violently pounded on the front door. "Open the damn door, Buttercup, or I'm going to be really pissed off. You don't want to see me pissed off, do you?"

Rhychard forced his eyes open and stared at the clock. Seven A.M. And the person at the door already sounded pissed. *:Kree?:* No answer. Great. Tryna was still off scavenging for information. Who knew where the giant mutt was. He hadn't returned after their foray into breaking and entering. Rhychard sighed. He was going to have to get up, and now *he* was pissed.

Throwing the sheet to the side, Rhychard grabbed one of the short swords from the harness and stormed his way to the front door. Well, it was more like stumbled, but he did it while he was fuming, so he felt like he was storming. As he left his room, he realized he hadn't slipped pants on and, as he knew he was wearing his giant Walmart smiley face boxers, he felt less like a powerhouse and more like an angry boyfriend. Hopefully, the sword would intimidate where his outfit wouldn't.

As he entered the living room he spotted Buttercup wearing one of his T-shirts and huddled in a corner, tears streaming down her face. Even from where he was he could see her body shaking. She was afraid. Very afraid. He gestured to the door. "Who?"

She wiped the tears from her cheeks with the back of her hand. Rhychard could see that she was trying to pull herself together and was failing miserably. It was understandable. It hadn't exactly been her best week. "It's Jerome…my pimp. He's the one who hooked me up with Pastor Adrian."

Well, that would explain how Jerome knew where to find her. If Vargas couldn't use the gargoyles to get her, Adrian would use humans. Rhychard wondered what Vargas had offered the preacher that would have him make such evil decisions. How could Rhychard have been fooled all this time by the man?

Jerome pounded harder. His screams were going to wake up the neighbors. Rhychard was already getting fussed at enough by the Condo Association. He didn't need any more complaints. He yanked the door open, grabbed Jerome by a handful of hair, and jerked him inside and down onto the floor, the point of the sword an inch from his Adam's apple. "I was trying to sleep!" He felt like an idiot from some Hollywood spoof, but the small man with the three days' worth of stubble wasn't staring at Rhychard's boxers. His eyes were glued to the sword.

The kid, and that's what he was really, a kid, was probably not even five and half feet tall standing up. He had shaggy hair that was in desperate need of a comb and a gazillion tattoos up and down his arms as well as around his neck. The man had biceps instead of brains and at the moment he had lost his bravado, as well. "What the hell, man?"

Buttercup stayed where she was, her body still shaking. Rhychard tightened his grip on the sword. "That's my question, as well. What the hell are you doing pounding on my door?"

"I came to get what's mine. Someone told me you kidnapped Buttercup." He tried to posture, puffing his chest out, but from where he lay sprawled on the carpet he just looked like an overturned turtle.

"What's 'yours'? She's not a watch. And I didn't kidnap Buttercup; I rescued her. And if you *were* rescuing her, why would you be pissed at her?" Rhychard cocked his head to one side as he dragged the sword's point down Jerome's torso and aimed it right at his crotch. The man probably valued that head over his upper one. "Buttercup is free to leave whenever she wants, but it's not safe for her out there right now. I would think you would want to protect your employees." Rhychard pressed the sword point into the man's jeans. "Never mind. She quits. Your life insurance policy really sucks and, well, she needs better benefits." He pulled the sword away and took a few steps back, still remaining between pimp and hooker.

Jerome pushed himself off the floor brushing off as if trying to wipe away his fear. He glanced at Buttercup with narrow eyes and Rhychard knew the man was blaming her for his loss of dignity. Rhychard knew how the streets worked. Buttercup had grown a conscience and started thinking for herself. That just wasn't allowed in their world. Jerome believed that he really did own her and was free to do with her as he pleased. Right now, what the man pleased was to hurt her for his wounded pride.

Jerome stood with arms at his sides, fists clenched. His eyes never left Buttercup. "Nobody quits."

Rhychard shook his head. "People quit all the time, and if I was you, I'd quit right now. I'd cut my losses and just walk away. Buttercup is under my protection and I'm very protective." He raised the sword, tip aimed at Jerome's chest. "Now, get out of here, and tell Adrian I said hello."

Jerome stared for a moment longer. Rhychard could tell he wanted to say something, but thought better of it as his eyes stared at the sword in the Warrior's hand. "I'll be back. No one quits Jerome." He turned and left, his back stiff and straight.

Not until Rhychard had locked and bolted the door did Buttercup come out of her corner. Her arms were wrapped around her chest, her hands rubbing up and down her upper arms. She still had that trapped look in her eyes.

"He's gone," Rhychard said as he walked over to where she stood.

Buttercup fell into him, her trembling body trying to wrap him around her like a blanket. He held her, the top of her head coming to his chin. He could smell his Irish Spring and made a mental note to pick up something more feminine for her. If she was going to be there for a while—and it looked like she was—she might as well have what she needed.

"I take it he didn't know you quit?"

With a deep breath, Buttercup pushed away from him, her thin fingers wiping the water streaks from her eyes. "I wasn't planning on quitting." She gave him a wan smile as she wrapped her arms around herself. "I was only quitting what I was doing for Pastor Adrian, but those creatures attacked and you saved my life and brought me here. I hadn't had a chance to talk to Jerome. I should have known, though. The pastor found me through him. If I quit one, I was disobeying the other. Jerome hates being disobeyed."

Rhychard nodded as he went to the kitchen to get her something to drink. The sink was empty of dishes. So was the drain board. "Hey, where are all of my glasses?"

"In the cupboard where they belong. Don't you ever clean?"

Opening the cupboard, he saw all of his dishes, clean and put in their proper place. At least, he assumed it was the proper place. He usually kept everything in the sink, rinsed off what he needed and then dumped it back when he was finished. He didn't see anything wrong with it. Kree ate out of a bowl and Tryna preferred to eat in privacy. Rhychard hadn't acted domesticated since, well, since Renny. He stared at the glass he held, his change in lifestyle very apparent to him all of a sudden. *You've let yourself go, ol' boy.*

He opened the refrigerator, took a look at the week old milk and decided on water. He needed to get to the store. Rhychard chuckled to himself at the notion of doing anything as mundane as grocery shopping. His life had become way too complicated.

Rhychard heard the familiar jingle of bells in his bedroom. Shopping was going to have to wait. He downed the tap water and refilled his glass before going to see what Tryna had discovered, handing Buttercup a glass of water on the way. She stayed on the couch staring out the sliding glass door.

As he entered his room, he saw Tryna standing by his bed, her head and shoulders the only part of her visible over the mattress. However, she was not alone. Towering beside her was an elf that caused Rhychard's blood to boil instantly. Kendalais. His long blond hair was tied back in a queue with leather dyed gold revealing his elven ears. His blond brows started upward over ocean blue eyes as he stared at the Warrior. The elven knight stood in glistening armor and Rhychard was very aware that he was still in his smiley face boxers. He could have sworn he noticed Tryna blushing, if faeries blushed, but he knew it wasn't because of him being in his skivvies in front of her. It was because of Kendalais. Elves put a lot of stock in formality and Kendalais was a well-respected knight, a Sidhe Warrior Master, which almost put him in the nobility. Of course, Rhychard could care less.

The Warrior walked the rest of the way into his room and plopped down on the bed. The Warrior Master's face tightened in consternation and Tryna glared at him. While Tryna had strong opinions about the way things were handled a couple of months ago, she still believed in the formal structure of the faerie world. He, however, didn't, and so he just smiled back. "Come to lend a hand?"

Kendalais rested a hand on the pommel of his sword, but the rest of him remained as a statue. "How you survive this boorishness, Tryna, I will never comprehend."

By the look on the faerie's face Rhychard knew he was in for a scolding on elven decorum and conduct, but it was worth it to get under Kendalais's skin. "He grows on you, Warrior Master."

Kendalais's lips curled. "So, he's like mold."

"Ah, but mold makes penicillin, so I'm the cure," Rhychard said.

"And yet, you behave like the disease."

Rhychard just waggled his eyebrows at the knight, smiling. Tryna had had quite enough, however. "It's amazing to me how two of the most talented Warriors I know can behave like little boys."

"He started it." Rhychard stuck his tongue out at the elf.

Tryna rolled her eyes at him. With a deep breath, she said, "Kendalais is here to assist us in stopping Vargas from opening a Gateway to the Nether. And Kendalais, Rhychard is the Warrior for this area, chosen by the Guardian. You both need each other at the moment, so I recommend you get along."

Rhychard glanced at the small faerie knowing she was right. As much as he hated the smug Sidhe Warrior Master, he needed his knowledge at the moment. There were lives on the line and Renny's was one of them.

With a nod of his head, Rhychard slid himself off the bed and stood to his feet. He didn't extend his hand in truce, but he did withhold the sarcastic comments. "So, what do we do?"

Kendalais crossed his arms over his chest, his back rigid. His face was still masked in arrogance, but Rhychard no longer cared. There was work to be done and he needed the smug bastard to accomplish it. The elf glanced at Tryna without turning his head. It was obvious that necessity was warring with his ego, but Rhychard was unsure how much time they had.

"Are you here to help or not?"

Kendalais cocked a slanted eyebrow. "Humans have no patience."

"Well, we don't live thousands of years, so time is a commodity we tend not to squander."

The Sidhe Warrior was about to open his mouth in rebuttal, but Tryna stopped him. "Please, Warrior Master, we must know what you know and have time to act on it."

The elf's nod was barely perceptible, but he wasn't one for grand gestures, anyway. "Tryna has told me of the demon's purpose and progress. The Void's influence on the land before and the weakening of the Way's impact to change that influence now has gained Vargas a solid footing on his attempt to open a Gateway to the Nether. The Void will destroy Harbor City if that were to happen, of course."

Rhychard suppressed his rage. "Of course."

Kendalais remained ignorant of Rhychard's annoyance. Elves were quite oblivious to human mannerisms, believing most of them the silly emotions of spoiled children. "He will require a large sacrifice, for a Gateway can only be opened with blood. Lots of blood."

"It's always blood with demons." Rhychard glanced out his window at the oaks behind his house.

"Life is in the blood, therefore, the power and energy of life resides in the blood. It has always been this way since the gods created life."

Rhychard turned back to Kendalais. "It's still pretty revolting. Is there a timeframe for this ritual?"

"During the time of the Dark Moon."

Rhychard glanced at Tryna, confusion on his face. With all of his dealings with faeries and demons and magic he should learn all these things eventually. Of course, what would Tryna have to do then?

Looking up at him, she merely said, "That's this coming weekend."

"The new Saturday night service. That place will be packed with people." It would be a captive audience for Vargas's slaughter. Rhychard glanced back out his bedroom window. This was not good. "How do we stop it?"

Tryna glanced up at the Warrior Master. Rhychard glanced from the faerie to the elf, knowing he needed to be patient, but not having it in him to hold on much longer. Kendalais uncrossed his arms and slid his hands inside his cloak as he walked over to the window and stared into the trees beyond. The elf stood silent for awhile, obviously trying to piece together his answer. He continued to stare out the window as he spoke. "It will not be enough to get the event cancelled. That will only delay the demon." Kendalais turned and stared at Rhychard. "You will need to allow the ritual to begin and then remove the source of his power before he can utilize it. In this way, the ritual will implode upon itself sending the power inward. The land will be ruined for future attempts as the power of the ritual flowing backwards will neutralize the negative life energy that is there, driving it deeper into the earth where it cannot be tapped."

Rhychard glanced at Tryna. She kept her eyes on Kendalais as she said, "Get the people out."

"Why didn't he just say that?"

"I did." Kendalais arched an eyebrow at him. "Once the ritual is started it cannot be halted. Anyone trapped inside, however, will be killed. If you cannot rescue enough people, then the ritual will succeed and a Gateway to the Nether will be opened."

Rhychard didn't much care for the word "implode," but it was better than the Void gaining an easy access route into Harbor City. The Warrior glanced down at the faerie. "Looks like I need to get my suit ready for church."

Tryna didn't smile.

Rhychard turned back to Kendalais. Tryna was stuffy enough, but with the Sidhe Warrior Master around, her formality was turned up to full blast. It made the human Warrior edgy. "Will you be hanging around to lend a hand?" Rhychard knew that what he needed and what he wanted were two different things at the moment. He wanted the pointy-eared Sidhe to just leave, hopefully to never return. However, he also knew that having Kendalais along for this fight would lean them more into the victory department.

The tall elf shook his head. "I cannot. There are problems elsewhere that I must attend to. I was almost out of the realm by the time Tryna's message reached me as it was."

Rhychard just nodded. This time he was on his own. He heard the shuffling of fabric beside him and glanced down at Tryna. Okay, so he wasn't totally alone. He had a two-and-a-half-foot faerie, a giant mutt, and an anorexic street walker. There was no reason in the world why they couldn't take on a powerful demon and his host of minions.

We're doomed.

Glancing down at Tryna, Rhychard knew it was time for him to leave. He bowed his head at the Warrior Master. "I wish you luck on your journey."

Kendalais arched an eyebrow, the only sign that the farewell was out of the ordinary for the human Warrior. With a slight bow of his head, the elf said, "I wish you luck on your journey, as well as victory in your battles."

Rhychard nodded once more and left his room. Tryna would think he was learning his place in the Land Under hierarchy. The truth was he just liked keeping Kendalais baffled. Of course, as Rhychard entered the hall for the second time that morning he wished he had grabbed some pants to put on. This day was not going well and he hadn't even had breakfast.

Seventeen

A gentle breeze came off of Manatee Creek, keeping the late-morning sun from becoming unbearable. A momma duck floated past trailed by seven little babies in a zig zag pattern. About three feet behind was baby number eight not seeming to care that it wasn't with the others. Rhychard took a pull from his Rocky Patel as he watched the loner stop here and there periodically to investigate some floating leaf or pesky insect. *Take your time and enjoy the sights, my friend. Things change all too quickly.*

The flat rock—his thinking rock as he liked to call it—was warming as the sun floated higher into the morning sky. The creek water lapped at it as it floated by, a harmony mixing with the rustling leaves above him. A mullet jumped off to the west. Rhychard tilted his head back and allowed the sun to warm his face. The heat helped cool the tension his morning had brought him, and there had been quite a bit of tension.

He heard the snap of twigs behind him. Out of reflex, he searched for the Guardian Sword, but it was just cold bronze. Of course, its timing hadn't exactly been spot on as of late. Vargas had said that the Seelie had lied to him. Sacred Ground wasn't really sacred and now the sword that was supposed to protect him was being picky about when it did or didn't pitch in. Were they hoping that Rhychard would get himself killed so they could be done with the human? If only they could take the damn sword back. He'd gladly be shed of it and them.

But he was stuck with it. He knew for a fact because he had tried, right here on the very rock upon he was perched. Tryna and Kree warned him it wouldn't work. Once the Guardian chose you, sword and Warrior were bonded until the Warrior died, much like the coshey when they chose a Warrior. Even Kendalais, who wanted nothing to do with a pathetic human, told Rhychard that to get rid of the sword was tantamount to committing suicide.

He didn't believe them. Back then he thought they were merely using him to fight their battles. He had stood on the rock he now sat on, the Guardian Sword in his hand and with all of his strength hurled it into the middle of the creek. He didn't stay to watch the ripples fade, but turned to make his way back to his condo.

He never made it out of the woods.

The air suddenly felt like it had been sucked out of him. It was as if he was the one sinking into the creek instead of the sword. Pain grasped his chest, squeezing its hot tendrils around his heart. He collapsed, curled up in a ball on the ground. He was going to die.

He wasn't ready to die.

He gasped for breath, fighting to suck air back into his lungs. He pulled his body back around to the creek and, fist over fist, hauled himself back to the rock. His hearing was gone. Even his gasps were silent. Dragging himself to the edge of the slab of rock, he dropped into the icy water and let himself sink. He knew he needed to regain the sword.

The water sucked him in, enveloping him in a cocoon of chilly darkness. He couldn't see. He couldn't hear. He couldn't breathe. But he could feel, and what he felt were tiny hands gripping his and pulling him out into deeper waters. Another set of fingers pulled at his other hand and he could feel even more pulling at his shirt and pants. He was being dragged downward and in the distance he made out the throbbing blue glow of the Guardian Sword.

Whatever—whoever—was guiding him was taking him right back to the sword. He pushed through the pain that was gripping him, ignored the fact that he was underwater surrounded by creatures he couldn't see, and swam for the sword. He kicked, his works boots heavy weights holding him back. Some of the tiny hands released their grip, his thrashing knocking the creatures away from him. He dove down. He stretched his hands out, reaching for the sword, reaching for his life.

He gripped the sword with his right hand and a surge of electrical energy singed through him. The pain that had been tightening around his muscles and organs, now shot outward like a million bee stings on every nerve. He screamed and then he breathed; only he took in the briny creek water instead of air. The hands gripped him again, pulling him upward to the surface. He choked. He tried to cough out the water, but more took its place. He panicked. He wasn't going to make it. After losing everything else, he was going to be found floating face down in the creek.

Rhychard felt himself being hurled upward and soon he heard himself choking, felt the warm air on his face. He kicked his feet, trying to float. The sword pulled him down; the weight of his boots didn't help. He forced himself to swim for the rock gripping the sword with all he had. He would not let go of it again.

Even in the murky water, he could feel the warmth of the Guardian Sword at the reconnection. Small hands helped him until he reached the flat rock and he pulled his soaked body onto the edge and collapsed, the sword still in his hand. His breathing came in gulps of air as he savored every breath, realizing how close he came to never taking another.

He rolled over after a time, forcing his aching muscles to move. He heard the musical pop of Tryna's arrival and her frightened "Rhychard!" as she ran the rest of the way to where he lay panting. It was then that he had discovered she was somehow attuned to him and could tell when he was in peril. He assumed the sword had some fancy magical GPS attached to it. The small ellyll used her magic to warm his shivering body. He hadn't been able to tell if he was trembling because of the creek or the fact that he had almost died. Both, more than likely.

Rhychard hadn't thought about that experience since it happened, trying hard to banish it from his memory, and his body shook with the remembrance. "You know, I never did find out what all of those little hands belonged to that day."

Tryna walked to the edge of the flat rock, her tiny hands clasped behind her. He had known it was her by the light footsteps. Kree's would have sounded like an elephant ravaging his quiet sanctuary. She must have walked from his condo as opposed to her usual popping appearance, which meant her mind had to be heavy with her conversation with Kendalais.

"Not what, but rather who. The naiads of the creek helped rescue you." Tryna stared down at the murky green waters of Manatee Creek. "When you tossed the Guardian Sword into this water, the separation of the bond of magic could be felt everywhere. Every creature of the Seelie knew that a Warrior had rejected his calling. The naiads waited here to assist you when you rescinded that decision."

"Naiads?"

"Water nymphs. They keep to streams, lakes, small rivers or creeks helping to protect the life within just as sylvans and dryads protect the trees and forests."

"I've never seen them." Rhychard still sat, but now his eyes were on the water. Nymphs lived in his creek. That was both scary and intoxicating all at the same time.

"You quite possibly never will. As with many in the faerie world, they have not yet decided what to make of you."

Rhychard didn't say anything. The truth was he didn't know what to make of them, either.

"Kree told me about your attempt at Harvest Fellowship last night."

Rhychard took a long pull from his cigar, allowing the mild smoke to linger before exhaling. He stared at the glowing tip as he recalled the fiasco of breaking into Adrian's office. "It was worth a try. Without the pastor's so-called evidence people can stand up to him. Too bad gargoyles can get onto church property now." He knew he sounded bitter, but he couldn't help it. Everything he had been told seemed to have been a lie.

Tryna nodded, her tiny childlike lips pressed into a stern line. "It is worse than I feared."

"We have another problem. Jerome, Buttercup's pimp, came looking for her. I had to convince him to leave."

"This is the man she works for?" She turned and looked at him, her brows bunched in a confused knot.

"Her boss, so to speak, yes. He didn't like the fact she wasn't working his streets. My guess is Adrian told him where to find her and Vargas told Adrian."

"That is unfortunate." Tryna turned back to the water.

He could tell that something was on her mind, but he wasn't going to pry. He was surprised she hadn't ripped into him about his behavior with Kendalais. The faerie world had their protocols and Tryna seemed to expect him to follow them. He wouldn't. He wasn't a damn elf and he refused to act like one. If they didn't want a human, then their Guardian should not have called one.

"Why did you do it?"

He stared at her small back, the breeze playing with the skirt of her burgundy dress. "Do what?"

Tryna turned and faced him, her blond hair framing her thin face. "Protect Buttercup. Why did you do it?"

"You wish I would have let him have her?" That seemed totally unlike the ellyll. If Tryna wanted him to abandon her, why rescue the girl in the first place?

"It is not. Yet, it does seem to be what you wish. Would this not fall under the same situation as helping Patricia Ivey? Did you not inform your friend, Trace Wheeler, you were no longer interfering in human affairs?"

I'm going to kick that mutt's ass. Rhychard looked away from Tryna and stared at the opposite shoreline of the creek. "It's kind of hard to avoid helping when the guy is pounding the hell out of my front door, waking up the whole complex."

"You could have just handed her over to him."

He snapped his head back around. "You want her killed? You know damn well what would happen to her if I let him take her." He flicked the end of his cigar into the creek. A small, feminine hand reached out of the water and threw it back. "What the…?"

Tryna shrugged. "Naiad's don't like water pollution or cigars." Rhychard picked up the soggy butt and was about to toss it over his shoulder when Tryna held up her hand and stopped him. "Dryads are just as particular."

Rhychard sighed, but held onto the soaked cigar. Tryna walked over and stared into his eyes, which were almost level with hers while he was sitting. "It is because of this deep concern of yours for others that the Guardian chose you. You cared about Buttercup's wellbeing and protected her. It's the same with Mr. Morsetti. His worry about his life mate finding out and not believing him isn't related to Vargas's plan to use the church to open a Gateway. Yet, you offered to talk to his life mate and make her understand. Furthermore, you did it knowing he was one of the ones that turned his back on you when Miss Saunders terminated her relationship with you."

Rhychard shook his head. "Remind me to talk to Kree about confidences between friends." He rested his arms on his knees, his fingers intertwined. He stared out at the water as it rippled around his thinking rock.

"Kree worries about your welfare. Vargas would have you believe we gave you false knowledge and I can comprehend how you would view it that way. But Warrior, I promise we have not been deceptive in our dealings with you. The Guardian Sword draws its power from you just as you draw power from it. Vargas can only step upon Sacred Ground when it ceases to be sacred. I cannot force you to believe or even to act to put an end to what is transpiring." The small ellyll stepped forward and put her tiny fingers over Rhychard's heart. "I know what is in here and I trust it to lead you in the proper course, even knowing how much your heart aches at present." She pressed on his chest once and then stepped away. "I trust you to do what is right, even if you don't trust yourself." With a jingle of bells, she vanished, leaving the Warrior alone with her words and his thoughts.

He still wanted to rip Kree a new one, but he knew the elven hound had been right in going to Tryna. Rhychard stood and walked to the edge of the rock, staring down into the murky water. He hadn't been himself lately and it turned his stomach. Even Trace was disappointed in him and that was saying quite a bit coming from the friend with no real priorities. The truth was he had done all he could to save his relationship with Renny. In the end, it had been her decision to end it and move on.

Rhychard held the wet cigar in his hand and gestured to the creek. "Sorry about the cigar. I'll be more thoughtful from now on." He started to turn and walk away, but just before he did a small hand rose out of the water and waved at him.

He had seen quite a bit in three months and still he was amazed at every new thing he was confronted with. He gave the naiad a small wave back as he turned and left. He needed to get Trace. They had somewhere to go.

Eighteen

"If there is no job, where are we going?"

Rhychard glanced over at Trace Wheeler, who was only slightly rough in appearance as opposed to his usual total mess. "To finish one."

The afternoon had started to make its slow slide into evening with the sun dipping toward the west. Shadows were getting longer and rush hour was starting to clog the narrow streets. Rhychard had called Trace and told him to be ready. Luckily, his friend was never into anything more important than the new level of Angry Birds and a Cheetos sandwich, so there was never a problem getting his help.

Rhychard could have done the job by himself, but since Trace had been the one to get the gig in the first place, he should be a part of its conclusion. Besides, Rhychard needed to redeem himself in the eyes of his friend.

It had taken Rhychard a while sitting on his Thinking Rock, but sense somehow seeped through his thick skull. Both Tryna and Kree had been right, and Trace for that matter. Bitterness was like a cancer that devoured a person's spirit and Rhychard had to shake it. Renny had made her choices. She had had the freedom that he had not been given to decide which path to follow and she had chosen not to walk with him. He could blame the Guardian, the sword, the elves, and the Void, but ultimately it had been her decision to walk out of his life. Tryna had only tried to help him, to keep him from ending up like Jamairlo, ripped to shreds in a dirty alley. Kree was the only coshey willing to be Rhychard's elven hound. The rest thought a human Warrior ridiculous and the sooner the Void did away with him the better. Kree had turned his back on his brethren and stood at Rhychard's side when he discovered none of the Seelie really wanted to be a part of a human Warrior. Kree now shared in the same ostracized status as Rhychard. Neither deserved his anger and scorn. They deserved his all and, from now on, they were going to get it.

As they turned into the Sky Wind subdivision, Trace shifted in his seat, a smile broadening his whiskers. He didn't say anything. He didn't have to. That childlike grin of his said it all and, as Trace grinned, so did Rhychard. He still wasn't sure what he was going to do, but it didn't matter. He was doing something and that felt good.

After Tryna left him at Manatee Creek, he had made several decisions. One was to make his own rules as a Warrior. The structure that had been set up centuries ago worked for the Sidhe, but Rhychard was not an elf. He lived on earth, not in the Land Under. The elves could follow their little code because they didn't interact with humans unless necessary. Rhychard had to constantly, because he was, after all, human. It was time to do things his way and if the elves didn't like it, it was simply too bad. They were stuck with him according to their rules and would just have to deal with it. The Guardian had chosen him, not the other way around.

After taking a couple of right turns, they could see the overabundance of the Ivey home ahead. Another moving truck was already parked at the curb in front of the house and its rear door was open wide. Patricia Ivey stood to the side, tears streaming down her face, her hands balled together as she pleaded with her son. Justin Ivey stood talking to two men wearing black shirts a size too small. By the scarred looks of them, both had mug shots floating in the system.

Rhychard pulled up right behind the other truck, blocking the bed of it, and turned off his vehicle. *That should slow them down a bit.*

"Hey! What the hell are you doing? You can't park there." One of the two thugs turned and started toward Rhychard, his finger pointing. Obviously, his mother had not taught him how rude that was.

Rhychard turned to Trace, the Warrior's smile replaced with a smoldering glare. "You're about to enter my world, Trace. Do you still want to help this lady?"

Trace slid back into his corner, a scared confusion scrunching his eyes together. "Yes."

Rhychard nodded. "Open the back of the truck and step back." The Warrior opened his door and dropped out of the truck. *Show time.* Trace had been slow to move. Rhychard turned to his friend as he reached over his shoulder and gripped the Guardian Sword. As he pulled it from its sheath, he could feel the power taking hold, the voices screaming for battle. Trace's eyes went wide as the sword materialized. "Move!" Rhychard yelled. He finished pulling the sword around as he turned back to the man bearing down on him.

Or had been. At the sight of the sword that hadn't been there a second before, the wall of a man stopped cold, his mouth frozen agape.

"Justin Ivey, you've been a naughty son." Rhychard grinned at the toothpick in a suit as he kept the sword pointed at the first of the heavier men. The second just stood, his eyes going from one to the other, not knowing what to do.

Rhychard heard the back door of his truck slide open followed immediately by Trace's scream.

:You could have at least warned him I was back there.: Kree padded around the corner of the truck and into sight. Miss Ivey screamed, as well, and everyone was backing up.

:Sometimes people have to see to believe.: Something like his life needed more than words to describe. It needed visual aids.

Kree jogged to the side of the driveway and sat on his back haunches. His silver tail flipped back and forth with slow sweeps as he stared at Justin. *:You most assuredly have this human's attention. He reeks of fear.:*

"You have no right to be here." Justin's voice was more a squeak than a threat.

Rhychard just smiled. "We didn't get paid for this job and I'm here to repossess." Out of the corner of his eye, he saw Trace walking over to Miss Ivey trying to calm her down. He probably needed her to calm him down just as much. To Trace it more than likely seemed as if one of his video games came to life.

"Repossess? You can't take something that's not yours." Justin took a step forward.

Kree lurched to his feet and took a couple of quick steps forward. Justin froze.

"Isn't that what you were just now doing?" Rhychard said. He then turned to the muscle Ivey had hired. "And since you two were going to help him, you will help me. I want everything loaded into the back of my truck." Holding the Guardian Sword straighter, he took a step toward the first man. With his most menacing tone, he simply said, "Now."

Both men glanced at Justin Ivey who was unable to do anything except stare at Kree. Without another word they started hauling boxes.

:The blond gentleman with the scar on his right ear is contemplating an escape.:

"Unless you want a matching scar on your other ear, I wouldn't even think about running. My furry friend here reads thoughts. He'll know what you are thinking before you do and then I'll have to use my pointy friend to teach you the error of wrong thinking." Rhychard stared at the cold bronze as if considering using it anyway. "It pays to have such good and talented friends."

One of the men, the one without the scar, turned and glared. "It's a sword, not a gun. What are you going to do? Throw it at us?"

Rhychard reached over his shoulder and pulled one of his short swords out of its sheaths. The man's eyes went wide. "I get the gun comment quite a bit, but in the end it doesn't matter. These aren't your normal swords, in case you hadn't noticed. But, please, run and let's see how far you get."

The burly man stared with dark eyes at both swords. Rhychard just shrugged and smiled. The man turned to his friend and gestured to the boxes, grumbling to Justin that he was going to suffer for their embarrassing labor. Justin paled even more, a feat Rhychard didn't think possible.

Every time Justin went to move, Kree growled him back into place. The man was beyond frustrated, but still too scared of the massive hound in front of him to do anything about it. "What do you want? You can't just take my things!"

"First, they are not your things. Second, we aren't taking them. Are we, Trace?" Rhychard glanced at his friend who had his arm around Miss Ivey in a protective gesture.

"No, we're not." Trace's voice held the strength his body wasn't showing. "We're taking Miss Ivey's possessions somewhere safe where you can't sell them." Trace turned and held the elderly lady's hands as he smiled at her. "And then, we're going to call her other children and tell them what's going on."

"I'm sure they're not going to be all too happy that you were trying to cash out your inheritance ahead of time," Rhychard said. He stood, following the movements of the others with his eyes, the two swords still gripped firmly in his hands.

Kree turned his head toward the back of the truck, a low growl building up from his stomach. "I told you," Rhychard called out. "Kree knows your thoughts. You are not going to make it far sneaking away on the side of the truck. Now, you're almost done. Why screw up now and get yourself killed?"

Kree swung his gaze back to Justin, still growling. "And, Justin, you can call the cops if you want, but really, Miss Ivey asked us to put her possessions back into storage. Isn't that right, Miss Ivey?"

Trace gave Patricia Ivey a squeeze around the shoulders. "It's okay. We're here to help. Nothing is going to happen to your belongings. I promise."

Miss Ivey looked into Trace's eyes, her own filled with unshed tears. Rhychard saw her nod and then take a deep breath. As she turned to her son, she stood a little taller. "These gentlemen work for me. Leave them alone."

Justin Ivey just glared at his mother.

:Perhaps we should endeavor to escort this offspring's mother with us when we vacate the premises.:

Rhychard didn't want to babysit someone else. Buttercup was enough of a house guest for the time being. Still, Kree had a valid concern. "Trace, why don't you take Patricia inside and let her call one of her other kids? It's time for a change of residence, I think." He heard the bay door of the truck slide shut. "We'll wait."

Trace nodded and then gestured the elderly Ivey to the house. Wiping the tears from her eyes, Patricia Ivey walked past her youngest son never glancing his way. She wore her fear like a cloak even after her little burst of bravado. Trace followed her, looking at Rhychard as he passed, his face a satisfied mask of gratitude, which gave Rhychard a warm sense of pride.

"It's loaded," the man with the scar on his ear said.

Rhychard searched the garage to make sure it was empty of everything they had originally stored inside. Satisfied that they had placed it all in the truck, he turned to the staring Justin and twisted the knife just a little more. "Pay them."

The blond man scrunched his face into incredulity. "Screw you. You made them do it; you pay them."

Rhychard stalked over to Justin. The two men just stood where they were, wanting to see what was going to happen. Rhychard was sure they wanted to run, but the promise of payment kept them in their place. Kree just sat still, his tongue lolling in the evening air.

As Rhychard neared Justin, the thin man did his best to straighten himself into some semblance of artificial toughness. His back may have been straight, but his body trembled. Rhychard brought the Guardian Sword up, the point right below Justin's chin, the voices begging him to strike the man down. He narrowed his eyes and growled through a feral grin, almost tempted to give into the Warriors of the past. "Now, Justin, you hired these hard working men to load a truck and they did. You don't want to rob them of their pay, do you?" To emphasize that he had better make the right decision, Rhychard pushed the sword tip into the man's pale throat drawing a pinprick of blood.

Justin held his head perfectly still as he reached into his back pocket for his wallet. His eyes never left Rhychard's as he held out the shiny leather bi-fold. Rhychard lifted the short sword back over his shoulder and slid it into its invisible harness. As soon as he let it go, the blade vanished, drawing gasps from everyone watching. He then took the wallet and held it out to the movers. "Take what he owes you." He then turned and glared at them. "And only what he owes you."

The taller of the two took the wallet, counted out three hundred dollars and handed it back. Rhychard took it and passed it back to the simmering Justin. To the movers, he just said, "Now, leave."

They didn't need to be told twice. Both men practically ran to their truck and it was pulling away before their doors were even closed. Rhychard couldn't say he blamed them.

Rhychard took the Guardian Sword away from Justin's throat, wiped the blood from the tip on the grass and then sheathed it. The voices silenced. As it vanished from sight, the Warrior walked over to Kree and scratched the coshey behind his ear. The elven hound closed his eyes and leaned into his hand, enjoying the attention. "Going to tattle tale on me?"

:Warrior, I am not an informant for the Seelie. I am a coshey. I am your elven hound. I chose you. I was not sent. My loyalty is to my Warrior.:

:Thanks, I needed to do this.:

Kree opened his eyes and swung his muzzle to glance up at Rhychard. His dark eyes revealed the depth of his care for the human. *:I know this. If I do not agree with something, I assure you I will be forthcoming with it. However, I will always support you. As you humans say, I have your back.:*

Rhychard scratched harder in gratitude. He needed the coshey's acceptance more than he realized. He had felt so alone since everything had happened to him. Yet, Kree had always been there. As had Trace and Tryna. He wasn't alone, just ignorant of those who had stuck by him.

-What are you intending to do with this one?-

-Not what he deserves.- Rhychard turned back to Justin. "You are to leave and not return before lunch tomorrow. Take no clothes. Just go. If you attempt to return before noon tomorrow, I *will* give you what you deserve. I promise." Rhychard took a deep breath when he realized his voice was getting lower and more of a growl. "Now go." Rhychard scratched Kree's head, waiting for Justin to move.

The youngest Ivey child just stood there for a minute, still trying to be defiant. In the end, he surrendered to what fate had punished him with, slid behind the wheel of his Beemer and left his schemes behind. Rhychard wasn't fooled, however. He knew the man would retaliate in some way. Hopefully, Patricia Ivey's other children were strong enough to keep him in check.

Trace returned with a much happier lady. Rhychard gave her his phone number as well as the storage unit and its combination so she could get all of her stuff when she was ready. Tears welled up in her hazel eyes again, but this time it was not due to fear. She wrapped her arms around Rhychard and clamped on. "Thank you, son. All I can say is thank you."

Rhychard hugged her back, feeling tears pooling in his eyes. He told her that Justin would not be returning until tomorrow and if he did she was to call Rhychard or Trace. She offered to pay them, but he refused. She had paid enough, already.

Trace and Rhychard climbed into the cab of the truck and Kree hopped into the back with the boxes. Everyone was quiet as they drove away, but the Warrior knew there would be questions. Trace was the first of his friends to know that there was something extremely different about Rhychard. Rules had been broken tonight. Not his, but those that Kendalais had tried to cram down his human throat, and Kree had stood by him through it all. That part had surprised him.

It had also empowered him to make his choices.

Trace sat, staring out the passenger window not seeing the houses passing by. "Thank you. For going back and helping her, I mean." His voice was soft, almost as if he was going to cry. "Thank you."

Rhychard felt his throat tighten as emotions welled up from within. He hadn't realized how far he had fallen from who he was. He had allowed his bitterness to hurt those people he truly cared about. "I'm sorry, Trace. I know I haven't exactly been myself lately."

Trace gave a weak chuckle as he turned and faced Rhychard. "You're not exactly yourself, now."

Rhychard nodded, laughing, as well. "I suppose you're right."

"So, what happened? Why do you wear invisible swords and what's with the giant dog back there?"

"Be careful, he can hear you. And he's not a dog; he's a coshey."

"He's back there. How can he hear me? And what's a coshey?"

Rhychard started at the beginning and told Trace the entire story. He went slow, answering each of his friend's questions, and there were quite a few questions. He was patient, explaining some things two or three times until the fog of confusion had turned to clear understanding. He was honest, admitting that he didn't completely understand it all and had questions of his own.

Kendalais had not been so patient. The Sidhe Warrior Master didn't care if Rhychard understood anything or not as long as he did what he was supposed to do. If it hadn't been for Tryna showing back up, Rhychard wouldn't know half of what he was sharing with Trace now.

When he finished recounting what had become his life for the past three months, the rest of the ride went by in silence. He knew Trace was processing it all. There was a lot to process. Rhychard wasn't sure how his friend would handle it or if he would even be his friend after hearing everything, but at least he knew the truth. That was all that mattered. He was through lying to people and hiding who he was from those around him. Trace was the first. Renny would be the second.

Nineteen

Rhychard sat astride his Suzuki and stared up at Renny Saunders's townhouse. The Friday sun had completely been swallowed by the cool quiet night. The sky was clear, the stars pinpricking the night canopy. It was the first night of the Dark Moon. Tomorrow that moon would hold power, power that Vargas would harness and use to open a Gateway to the Nether.

Rhychard still wasn't sure how he was going to stop the Unseelie demon or if he even could, but he did know he was going to tell Renny the truth. He didn't think it would change anything between them, but she would know he hadn't cheated on her. That was all he wanted at this point, to clear his name in her eyes. He hated that she thought bad of him, especially since he hadn't really done anything wrong.

Except not trust her. He should have told her everything from the start and not hid it from her no matter what Kendalais had commanded. Four years they had been together and he had listened to some pompous elf he had only known for a short time. That was what he had done wrong and what he was going to fix. Tonight. He was through doing things the Seelie way. He was doing things his way from now on and the elves could be damned if they didn't like it.

Renny was home. He had seen her car. The lights in her apartment were low, but on. His watch told him it was nine, but if Renny was still his Renny, she had a glass of Moscato in one hand and a Lisa Jackson novel in the other while she was curled up on the couch with her favorite afghan draped over her legs. Soft jazz would be playing through the house as the tendrils of smoke from several candles wafted their sweet aroma throughout. It was how they had spent most of their evenings. Quiet and together.

He wondered if Adrian came over and cuddled with her on the couch. Rhychard didn't doubt that the pastor could lie his way out of his home for a rendezvous with Renny, but would he treat her with the same tender care that Rhychard had always shown her? Rhychard wanted her happy and no matter how he looked at it he could find no way that she could be satisfied with the pastor. For one thing, Adrian couldn't be committed to her. He was already married. There were no dinners out, no weekend getaways. What could a cheating husband possibly offer her that would keep her hanging on? It made no sense, especially since she had dumped Rhychard because she thought he had cheated on her. Wasn't that a double standard? Hypocrisy?

He closed his eyes and took a deep breath. He couldn't allow his thoughts to travel that path. It was her life. They were her choices.

He slid off his bike, took a deep breath and crossed the street to her townhouse. He had to make her listen to him, to believe him. He had to convince her not to go to the church tomorrow night. He might not be able to save the congregation or even himself, but he'd be damned if he was going to allow her to be killed, as well. He had promised to protect her. That's what he was going to do whether she liked it or not.

He took the steps two at a time, eager to have the confrontation over, and he knew it would be a confrontation. Renny had made it quite clear that she wanted nothing to do with him. Ever. Again. He had to convince her to listen to him, at least one more time.

Rhychard took another breath as he straightened his coat and his back. With determination as well as desperation filling him, he knocked on the wooden door. He could hear the soft music inside and silently prayed it would help keep her calm.

Renny opened the door, took one look at him, and went to shut it again. "Go away."

Rhychard put his foot across the threshold, blocking the door from closing. "Please. I just need a few minutes and then, I promise, I'll go away for good if you want me to,"

"I've already told you I wanted you to go away. For good." Renny looked at his foot, then up at him. "If you don't move your foot, I'll break it. Now, go away."

"I know you don't want anything to do with me. I get it. Really. But please, just hear me out. I can explain everything. After all we've been through, don't you want the truth?"

"You've suddenly developed a conscience and want to confess? It's too late. I'm not interested." She was talking and not trying to slam the door on him. That was something, at least. Her long blond hair was pulled back into a ponytail and all she wore was an old Florida State T-shirt. His T-shirt. He ignored her creamy bare legs and focused on her eyes. She was wearing his shirt to lounge in. Soft music was playing and a quick glance inside at the coffee table showed a paperback propped open and a glass of white.

Rhychard tried not to smile, but his heart gained hope. He glanced back into her eyes and, behind the anger, he could see the hurt, hurt he had caused without ever meaning to. "Look, I know I don't deserve it, but please just give me a chance to explain and I swear I'll stay out of your life. After four years, can't we at least talk for ten minutes? Please."

"Four years didn't keep your pants up. Why should I want to spend ten more minutes with a cheater?"

He wanted to snap back that she was giving more than ten minutes to an adulterer now, but he knew that would get his foot broken for sure. He couldn't allow himself to get angry and lose control at this juncture of the journey. Renny's life was worth more than his pride. "This just isn't about me, Renny. It's more important than that. Please. I just need to explain."

He could see the struggle going on within her. He couldn't really blame her. Still, he had to convince her. "Please, Renny. I swear I'll never bother you again."

She stared at him and he could see her interior melt even if her exterior remained cold as ice. "Fine. A lifetime of peace is worth ten minutes of you." She held a finger up, pointing at his face as she narrowed her eyes. "But I swear, Rhychard, if you start in about Adrian, I'll kick you back out and call the cops telling them you broke in."

Rhychard held his hands up in front of him as if in surrender. "Not a word about your relationship. Promise."

She stared a moment longer as if contemplating whether she believed him or not. Finally, she just nodded once and opened the door allowing him to enter. "Your ten minutes starts now."

Rhychard stepped through the door, hearing her close it behind him. He inhaled deeply of the apple cinnamon candles she had burning. Emotions tugged at memories of his heart, but he shoved them down. He didn't have the luxury of time to wax nostalgic. Besides, a trip down memory lane may just get him tossed out on his ass. No, the clock was ticking and he needed to get her to understand the importance of the situation.

Turning, he slid his hands into his coat pockets. His courage was quickly evaporating. He had lived what he was about to tell her and he still didn't believe it. How on earth would he convince her?

"Do you remember about three months ago when I was moving that lawyer's office from its old building to its new location on Washington?"

"Yeah. You disappeared for three days. You never called or even offered a decent explanation for why you had vanished. Was that the first night you cheated on me?"

Rhychard closed his eyes and took another deep breath. *You need her to listen, Rhychard. Don't fight.* "No. But, that was the night everything changed. I know you're going to doubt what I'm about to say, but hear me out. I can prove it."

Renny crossed her arms and just stared at him as she arched her eyebrows.

"Oookay. The night started when I got held up by a train and then I heard someone scream. I went to investigate and wish I would have stayed in the truck." Rhychard told Renny how he had come upon the gargoyles attacking Jamairlo. He explained how he had felt a strong compulsion to get involved and how he had joined in the fight and even killed a couple of the gargoyles himself. He told her about his last conversation with the elf and Jamairlo making him promise to hold onto the Guardian Sword until another elf appeared. He described his fear and how Kendalais arrived and announced Rhychard as a Warrior of the Way. He held nothing back no matter how crazy he knew it sounded. This was his last effort to get her to understand what had actually taken place. "I still don't understand half of what's happening to me, no matter how great of a teacher Tryna is. Most of it scares the hell out of me, to be honest, but I have no choice. The sword is a part of me now."

Renny laughed. "That's an elaborate tale to cover up the fact you were sleeping with whoever this Tryna is. Life is full of choices, Rhychard, and you choose to continue to lie to me. Now get out. Your time is up." She started to turn toward the door, but stopped when he called out for her to wait. She glanced back at him, her expression daring him to continue his wild story.

Rhychard let out a heavy sigh. Words were not going to be enough. He couldn't blame her. He knew how it sounded. There was nothing else to do. With a deep breath of resignation, he reached over his shoulder to where he knew the pommel of the Guardian Sword would be and pulled it from its sheath. Renny's eyes went wide as it materialized. She stepped back, closer to the door as if ready to bolt.

"Renny, I am not lying to you."

"How…how did you do that?" She tucked a stray strand of hair behind her left ear. Her eyes never left the sword.

"The faerie put a spell on it to hide the sword unless I was holding it. It works only when I'm wearing it and I almost always have to wear it."

"I'm not talking about your faerie fixation. It's a magic trick you learned. I'm not buying it."

"Not buying it? Renny, this isn't a quarter I'm pulling from behind your ear. There are no trick mirrors or hidden doors. This is a real sword. The elves are real. All of this is real and very serious. People have died. More are going to. You can be one of them if you don't believe me." Rhychard allowed the sword to hang by his side. He didn't need her thinking he was going to kill her.

"What? Not believing you is going to kill me? Get out, Rhychard. Take your magic trick and get out."

"Not believing me isn't going to kill you. Vargas and Adrian are going to kill you and everyone at Harvest Fellowship if you don't believe me."

"That's it! I told you not to bring Adrian up. Get out! Now!"

Rhychard just stared at her. This wasn't working and he was finding it hard not to get into a shouting match with her. He forced himself to take a deep breath and try to cool his simmering temper. She wasn't making it easy. He had thought for sure seeing the Guardian Sword would have convinced her to believe him. How could she think it was only a stupid magic trick? "I said I wouldn't talk about your relationship and I didn't. I think keeping people alive is more important."

She glared at him. "Get out." It was practically a snarl.

He had failed. It had been his only chance and he had screwed it up along with everything else. "Renny…"

"Out!" She jerked a pointed finger at the door as she burned him in place with her eyes.

Just as he was about to give up, Rhychard heard the familiar jingle and pop that he had become so accustomed to. It had never sounded so beautiful, even if it did make Renny scream as she tripped over herself and fell hard on the floor.

Tryna walked over to where Rhychard stood. "Rhychard, don't be rude. Assist Miss Saunders back to her feet." The small ellyll stayed where she was as Rhychard crossed the distance, offering his hand to the fallen woman. "I'm terribly sorry, my dear. I did not mean to frighten you."

Renny ignored Rhychard's hand and just stared at the small faerie. "What are you?"

"I am an ellyll; a faerie, I believe you would say. My name is Tryna and you really do need to listen to Rhychard." The small faerie folded her hands in front of her as she looked into Renny's eyes, which for the moment were almost level with her own.

:The Warrior does not deceive you. You are in danger.:

Renny screamed again as she searched for the owner of the voice in her head. Rhychard knew that fear. He had felt it.

"What's happening? What's going on? Who is that talking?" Renny ignored Rhychard's help.

:Where are you?: Rhychard sent to Kree. *:Why are you here? Isn't this a break in the rules?:*

:No more so than a human Warrior. Tryna and I knew you would come here and have made the decision to assist you in your attempt to reveal your true nature to your former life mate.:

"The voice you hear, Miss Saunders, is that of Kree, a coshey bonded to Rhychard," Tryna explained as Rhychard gave up on helping Renny to her feet and went to open the door. "He is rather large, but harmless. Please do not be afraid."

Rhychard opened the door and Kree squeezed his way inside followed closely by Buttercup. The giant coshey padded his way to the far side of the room to lessen the intimidation of his size. Rhychard could tell it wasn't working, even with the honey-colored lady at the elven hound's side. Rhychard wasn't sure what had made Buttercup join the others or why they weren't more worried about her safety, but he found himself glad she was there. She smiled her reassurance at him, but remained silent.

Renny's mouth was open in a scream though no sound came out. She crab-walked backwards against a far wall and tried to push her way through the drywall.

Rhychard walked over and scratched Kree behind the ears. The elven hound pushed his head into the scratch. "He really is harmless, unless you're a pepperoni pizza, that is." *:Thank you, my friend.:* Rhychard turned to Renny, but stayed where he was. "These are my friends. They've saved my life as well as the lives of others. Tryna is the one you heard me talking to that night, and it was about me saving the police captain, John Relco. Renny, I have never lied to you or cheated on you. I just couldn't explain everything that happened to me. To be honest, I still can't. They are going against rules that have been passed down over thousands of years to help me convince you of what is really going on. You have to believe me, Renny. Your life does depend on it."

Renny sat there for a moment, staring. Rhychard just waited, giving her time to process what she was seeing; what she was hearing. He knew the shock it generated. Her living room had become a living fantasy novel. Yet, thanks to his friends, she had to believe him. He was serious when he said her life depended on it.

She sat there for a few moments taking deep breaths, staring at the floor. Everyone remained still, quiet. Finally, she pushed herself up against the wall and to her feet. She glanced around her apartment as if making sure it was still there, avoiding looking at the small group filling her place. She was still having trouble believing.

Patiently, Rhychard waited. Renny ran a hand over her hair as she tried to gain some composure. When she did speak, she directed her words at the only one yet to say anything. "And what kind of magical creature are you?"

"I'm not. I'm just a prostitute who got stuck in the middle of this mess. These people saved my life, the life your boyfriend tried to end."

Rhychard shot Buttercup a look, but she ignored him. He was worried more bad words against Adrian would set Renny off again. Buttercup apparently didn't care. "What Rhychard has told you is true and he hasn't even told you most of it."

Renny's eyebrow arched when Buttercup used the term prostitute and he could feel her scrutinizing gaze flicking between Buttercup and him. He didn't need her distracted. "No, we're not sleeping together. I haven't seen anyone since you."

"He's too busy whining about you leaving him to look at another woman." Buttercup stood with her arms across her chest. It was quite obvious she was not impressed with Rhychard's ex.

Renny's face flushed and she looked away. He hadn't meant it to be a jab, although Buttercup probably did. Still, it was the truth. He had pined away for her while she jumped into bed with a married man. Truth was truth and sometimes that truth hurt.

Renny turned back to Buttercup and Rhychard could see the challenge in her eyes. "No offense, but why would Adrian want to kill a prostitute?"

Buttercup lifted her eyebrows. "What? I'm not worth killing?" Rhychard gave her another look and she simmered down—a little. "Pastor

Adrian had me sleeping with men, so that he could blackmail them. That's how he's been able to accomplish everything at his precious church."

"That's true, Renny," Rhychard said. "You can ask David Morsetti if you don't believe me."

"She slept with David?" Her voice was a mixture of shock and disgust.

"No, actually it was David that convinced her to quit doing as Adrian wanted. That's why Adrian wants her dead." Between them, Rhychard and Buttercup explained her role in Adrian's subterfuge and how they rescued her that Saturday at the lake. That tale led them to an explanation of Vargas, the Void, and how the Unseelie were trying to open a Gateway into their city. As the story progressed Tryna added the details and knowledge, giving definition to things Rhychard struggled with while Kree decided to remain silent, having startled Renny enough as it was.

Rhychard's ten minute allotment turned into just over two hours. At some point the standoff ended and everyone took a seat on the couch or loveseat, Tryna sitting on the edge with her thin legs dangling down. Rhychard caught Renny staring at the small ellyll, not exactly sure what to make of the faerie. He knew what she was going through. He had gone through it. So did Buttercup. It was not something humans were used to. Faerie tales don't come true.

Yet, here they were smack dab in the middle of one.

"I can't believe he would do this." Renny tried to make every excuse possible for Adrian, but in the end and after tears of denial, she had to hear the truth. Pastor Adrian Michaels was quite literally leading his flock to Hell.

Rhychard felt sorry for her. Her world had basically been turned upside down twice. He also had to admit to being jealous that she was crying over the scumbag. She had truly fallen for the man and Rhychard had to admit it pissed him off. "We're going to stop them, Renny, but I need you to not be there. It isn't safe."

"Maybe I can talk to people, convince them of what is going on?" She looked hopeful.

"Like you believed me without the visuals?"

"Miss Saunders," Tryna said in her soft, musical voice, "people are very loyal to their spiritual leaders, even those who ultimately serve the Void. They have done great evil in the past, believing those above them truly spoke the words of their deity. You will not be able to convince them in less than the time given us."

"Even if you convinced a handful, there is still enough to suit Vargas's plans," Rhychard said. He dropped down to his knees in front of her and took her hands into his. He looked up into her emerald eyes, his own pleading with her. "Please, Renny. Tomorrow night you have to stay home. Please. For me."

Tears filled her eyes as she gazed down at him. He wanted to cry at what they had lost, but if she would stay home perhaps there was a chance to fix it all. She knew the truth of everything now. And she believed him.

She pulled her hand from his and placed it along his cheek, her touch warm and gentle. "I'm sorry, Rhychard, so sorry I didn't trust you enough to believe in you."

He squeezed the hand that remained in his, too choked up to speak. Instead, they cried their hurt away; lost in an embrace he had missed and thought he would never feel again.

Twenty

After the others left, Rhychard and Renny talked well past midnight. She had question after question and he patiently gave her the answers she needed if he had them. Some he just didn't have replies for, but he promised to get them from Tryna or allow Renny to ask her herself. She wasn't sure she was ready for another face-to-face with the faerie world, though. He didn't push her. This had to be at her pace. He was just happy she agreed to skip the Saturday night service and avoid Adrian until it was all over. She was going to go stay at her parents, so that the pastor wouldn't find her at home.

By the time Rhychard left her apartment, he was feeling much better about where he stood with Renny. If things went right, perhaps they could even get back together. That would finally get his mother off his back.

And make his world a brighter place.

"Don't get too far ahead of yourself, Rhychard," he said to himself, stepping out of the townhome entrance and into a humid Florida night. The absence of a moon in the night sky only reminded him of what he yet had to face. Not many knew how dangerous that moon could be or the power it gave certain periods. Like him, they just thought it was pretty.

It was far more than pretty. It allowed those who knew how to wield its magical energy to be deadly.

He gave the night sky one more glance as he slid into the saddle of his Suzuki. That moon was part of his headache this weekend. The light in Renny's apartment went out and Rhychard found himself staring at it with rejuvenated hope. The moon's chaos was worth it if it allowed Renny and him to be together again.

Now, he just had to survive the fight with Vargas.

Rhychard pushed the switch and cranked the throttle. It was time he got some rest, finally. And he knew that, even with a battle ahead of him, that night he would sleep like newborn puppies. Everything in his personal world was starting to right itself again. Trace. Renny. His anger and bitterness. He wondered if that was due to the moon, as well. If so, it was a fair trade-off.

A blast of heat scorched his back, almost making him lose control of the motorcycle. He swerved, almost taking out a parked car before being able to right himself and keep going. The sword's warning system was back, as well, it seemed.

Another bike pulled up on his right. One on his left. Shadows passed overhead and he knew gargoyles were near. He shot a glance at the motorcyclist on his left and noticed the grayish-blue tint of his hands. A look at the one on the right revealed the same thing. Dark elves. He was being ambushed. Visions of Jamairlo's tattered body flashed in his mind and somehow he knew how the Sidhe Warrior had felt. Rhychard knew he was going to die, and he was going to die alone. Kree and Tryna had escorted Buttercup back to the apartments. They were too far away to help. It was just him. He wondered who the Guardian would call next and could picture the smug look on Kendalais's face. "I knew the human would fail quickly."

The streets were quiet, most of the bars having already closed for the night. Rhychard let up on the throttle and tapped the brake. The dark elves pulled away a few lengths before they noticed he had almost stopped. As he saw their brake lights come on, Rhychard hit the throttle and roared past them, putting distance between the dark elves and him. He was too exposed where he was. While he might be able to take the elves in a fight, the gargoyles would rip him open from above. He needed to get closer to Whispering Oaks and help if he was going to survive the night.

If Vargas called out the evil Sidhe, he had to be feeling threatened. Perhaps his raid at the church had scared the demon. Perhaps the Destroyer had had enough of a human meddler.

:Kree!: Nothing. He knew the coshey could hear over distances, but there was a limit. He had to get closer.

The dark elves were catching him. A gargoyle swooped down and Rhychard had to duck to save his head. He hit the throttle harder and banked the next turn. He needed a street with trees overhead to slow the gargoyles down.

A Firebird pulled out of the street ahead of him and hit the brakes. He watched as a man leaned out of the passenger window, a gun pointing at him. Jerome. *I knew that bastard was going to show back up.* A shot fired as Rhychard swerved more to the driver's side of the car. One of the elves caught up beside him as Jerome fired off another round. Rhychard hit the brake, jerking himself back. The elf shot forward, the bullet hitting him in the shoulder. The creature was knocked into a spin and his cycle hit the ground, both skidding in a spin onto the sidewalk and into a light pole. A strong whine filled the night, sounding almost like a...*horse?* Obviously, elves don't take their bikes in for servicing. Jerome kept firing.

Rhychard hit the throttle again and took the next right. Gargoyles dove at him as he heard the brakes of Jerome's car being slammed. The other dark elf stayed with him. The Warrior was losing track of where he was. Was he getting closer or further away from help?

:Kree!:

He was on a small two lane road. There were fewer lamp posts and stop signs had replaced traffic lights. He was getting further away from the city proper. Not the direction he wanted to go. He needed to turn around, but gargoyles lined every side street, blocking him. He was being funneled somewhere, but where?

He glanced behind him. The dark elf was right on his rear. Jerome's car was closing the gap, as well. Ahead was the only direction to go, but he was sure he didn't want to go there. He had to get off the street he was on.

Rhychard reached over his shoulder and gripped the Guardian Sword. He felt the warmth of its power filling him as he drew it from its sheath and brought it forward, the voices screaming for action. He wasn't sure his idea would work, but a fight where he was had to be better than where they were leading him. The minute he was hurt Tryna would know and send Kree. He didn't want to get hurt.

As Rhychard neared the next intersection he swung out to the left, then made a hard right turn. He aimed his front tire at the gargoyle on the left. The creature jumped upward, into the air, its wings pounding the air. The other beast lunged at the Warrior only to catch the sword across his left shoulder. The blade sliced in and lodged into the creature's body, eliciting an agonizing screech. Rhychard held tight, expecting to be yanked off the Suzuki. Just as he felt himself being jerked backward, the beast exploded into a storm of ash. The motorcycle swerved and jerked and Rhychard had to fight to keep it upright.

The other gargoyle screamed into the night and dove for Rhychard's back. In the distance, he heard the chasing vehicles make the turn and Jerome's gunfire echoing off the surrounding buildings. Rhychard hugged his bike and hit the throttle. He took the next right, heading back the way he came.

Where to, Rhychard? He didn't know. As long as the Unseelie air support was tracking him, his location would always be known. Rhychard felt a panic in his heart. How had they known where he was to begin with? He had just left Renny's. They had to have been there. They must have picked up his trail from her townhouse. It was the only thing that made sense. If they hurt her, he swore he'd…

Two gargoyles dropped low in front of him, making him almost drop his bike. Rhychard slashed at them with his sword as he leaned to the side of his motorcycle. He caught one of the gargoyle's legs and it exploded. This was going to be a long night if he couldn't shake the flying beasts. He was going to have to fight, but he needed to pick the battlefield.

Up ahead he spotted a parking garage for a medical complex. It would at least keep the gargoyles from attacking him from above. He took another swat at one of the leathery beasts as it swooped down on him and then hit the throttle. The gargoyles and remaining dark elf weren't going to be the problem. Jerome and his guns were.

Rhychard drove through the wooden arm blocking the entrance. Splinters flew everywhere as he apologized to his motorcycle. He hit the ramp and squealed around the first two turns. The dark elf lost distance in the turn, but was still close, and Jerome's Firebird finished the security arm as it busted in bringing up the rear. One of the gargoyles didn't duck fast enough and the concrete ceiling took off his head, turning it into a ball of ash.

The parking garage only had six floors, the sixth having no roof. Suddenly, he felt like he had chosen the wrong battlefield. As he cleared the second floor and hit the ramp to the third, he knew he needed to do something drastic. He just wasn't sure what.

As he made the left turn at the top of the ramp, the dark elf raced up it. He was gaining distance. Jerome was only a car length behind the Unseelie and gargoyles, four of them, flew above the others. Rhychard banked the next turn, putting as much speed as he dared into it. Instead of taking the next ramp up, however, he circled the third floor. As soon as he made the next left turn, he did a doughnut and headed back the way he came, stopping behind a burgundy Town and Country. It was time to get rid of some of his pursuers.

He leaped from his motorcycle, sliding the Guardian Sword back into its sheath. He reached inside of his coat for the iron knives he knew were there as he watched the turn through the tinted windows of the van. The ramp to the next level was only wide enough for two cars to pass, one in each direction. The dark elf would recover quickly, but Jerome and his goon would take a little longer. The first ones to have to go would be the flying monkeys.

The dark elf hit the ramp, cranking the throttle when Rhychard wasn't in sight, assuming the human had already made the next level. One of the gargoyles trailed him. Rhychard saw the headlights of Jerome's Firebird as it made the turn. Two gargoyles flew above. If he timed this right, he might be able to take out the dark elf's path.

The Firebird made the turn. The final gargoyle came into sight and Rhychard stepped out from behind the van, drew back his arm and sent the knife into the gargoyle's side. The beast screamed, its shrill shriek reverberating off the concrete walls before it exploded in a storm of ash. As he stepped to the bottom of the ramp, Rhychard saw the brake lights of the red vehicle, heard the squeal of tires locking up. The gargoyles above it cried out in rage as they spun in midair and dove toward the Warrior. Another knife was thrown, this time piercing the creature's bowels. The result was the same.

Rhychard heard Jerome screaming at his driver as the man tried to turn the car around. *I really should carry a gun for fighting humans.* The third gargoyle created a gust of wind with his wings. Rhychard's jacket flapped in the sudden tornado of air just as he was about to go for another knife. Throwing it with accuracy in the gargoyle's created wind storm wouldn't be possible, so Rhychard reached behind him and pulled the short swords from behind his back. As he did, he charged at the third gargoyle. The gray beast shrieked and folded its wings in on its sides as it dove at the advancing Warrior, talons out. Rhychard swung, keeping the razor sharp claws from connecting. Images of Jamairlo's shredded body filled his mind as he ducked under the gargoyle's talons and gave a backward swing of his sword. The gargoyle flew up and out of reach as it turned to face its victim. A shot rang out, missing Rhychard, but hitting the beast in the shoulder. It screeched at Jerome in anger, and then dove at Rhychard again. The Warrior hit the ground, rolling under the gargoyle as another shot echoed off the walls. This one caught the gargoyle in the wing, jerking it around. Rhychard wasted no time. Leaping to his feet, he drove his short sword into the creature's back. A shriek filled the air followed by ash.

Rhychard sheathed the short swords and drew the Guardian Sword. Jerome hopped out of the Firebird, firing shot after shot at Rhychard. The magic sword deflected each one, sending it safely into the concrete. The driver abandoned the car, which was now blocking the ramp completely, and fired his own 9mm. *Okay, this part I didn't consider.* Rhychard kept the sword upright in front of him, its power drawing the bullets to it and sending them off to either side.

The dark elf heard the fighting and returned. However, his motorcycle was blocked by the Firebird. Yet, he wasn't slowing. Rhychard stared. The elf was going to crash into the car and didn't seem to care.

The two humans kept coming for him, keeping him from doing anything but blocking bullets. This wasn't working out the way he had wanted.

As the dark elf aimed for the passenger side of the car, Rhychard watched as the Unseelie seemed to jerk the front tire into the air. The motorcycle shimmered as if it was being seen through a haze and Rhychard watched as the bike transformed into a black steed leaping over the abandoned car. "What the…?" *Tryna obviously has forgotten to tell me some things.* This plan was getting worse and worse.

The final gargoyle careened the corner in the air and followed the elf. At least, the other gargoyles were gone. Of course, he also gained a magical horse. Or was it a magical motorcycle? He didn't need inanimate objects changing into things!

Another shot fired and Rhychard angled the Guardian Sword so that the bullet ricocheted back at the driver. The man screamed as the round took him in the shoulder causing Jerome to turn and look. The pimp caught sight of the dark elf and the night black steed and he froze.

Rhychard didn't wait. He charged the short man, drawing back the sword as he went. Jerome turned, hearing the Warrior's boots, and brought the gun back up. Too late. Rhychard swung with both hands on the hilt, severing Jerome's arm and slicing halfway through his chest. "I told you to go away," Rhychard spat as he jerked his blade from the dead pimp.

As Jerome's body hit the ground, the dark elf was upon him. Rhychard had enough time to parry a thrust, keeping him from becoming a Warrior shish kabob. He backed up quickly, trying to regain his breath. The black stallion cantered to Rhychard's other side, trying to put him between horse and elf. The gargoyle hovered in the air just in front of him. He had had worse odds.

"So, your motorcycle has some great horse power." Rhychard continued to back up as they drew closer. "Do you put oats in the tank or does the horse drink gasoline? I'm a little confused as to how it all works."

The elf moved sideways, his feet crisscrossing as he moved. He swung his sword back and forth with one hand. His skin was a bluish gray. His pointy ears poked through his mane of white hair, and his red cat eyes were narrowed slits as he stared at Rhychard, waiting to cut him down. He wore dark pants that looked like they were costumes from Little House on the Prairie and a coarse long-sleeve tunic. He had leather boots with points that matched his ears. His fingers had nails that seemed like mini daggers. It was almost as if he were a miniature version of Vargas.

"If it's a secret, I understand," Rhychard said as he darted his eyes back and forth, trying to keep all three of his attackers in sight. "Does he talk? My coshey does this mind thing where he speaks inside your head. It can be annoying, at times, because he reads your thoughts. I'm really glad my girlfriend can't do that. You know, what I mean?" Rhychard reached over his shoulder and drew one of the iron swords. He kept the Guardian Sword pointed at the elf and the short sword at the stallion. "Not much for talking, are you?"

The elf grinned, his perfect white teeth pointy and sharp. His lips were a metallic color as was his tongue. "I see no reason to give you knowledge you will not need since I am about to kill you. The ellyll are a shortsighted race and you will always be poorly informed." He plunged, stabbing his sword at Rhychard's middle. The Warrior parried, knocking the elf's sword to the right. The elven steed's whinny was more like a shriek as its shadow covered Rhychard. He spun, swinging the short sword, slicing through the creature's stomach. The black steed shrieked as its middle opened and its intestines hit the dirty concrete.

Rhychard leaped to the falling beast's right, just barely missing the elf's sword, which instead hit the gargoyle that tried to drop down on Rhychard. The elf's sword not being made of iron, the gargoyle merely wailed. Rhychard swung his short sword around, catching the creature's waist. The wail was cut short.

Turning, Rhychard faced the Unseelie elf, both swords held before him. His breathing was ragged as the exertion from the fight, as well as the drain from the power of the sword, hit him. "Feel like talking now? Sorry about killing your motorcycle. There is a good bus system here in town you can use."

The elf glared at him. Rhychard knew he couldn't leave. He wasn't a gargoyle, the dogs of the Unseelie Court. He was a dark elf, equal to the Seelie Sidhe. Vargas would have him killed if he returned alive without killing the Warrior. This battle was not over. Not by a long shot.

"Still not talking? Let's see, the score is Warrior eight, dark creepy elf zero, and that doesn't count those I killed before we got here," Rhychard said. He needed time to catch his breath. "That's right, right? Let's see, four gargoyles, two humans, one pointy-eared elf and a motorcycle." Sirens sounded in the distance. *Great.* "You even stabbed one of the gargoyles, so maybe we can give you half a point. See, not a complete shut out."

The elf screamed as he brought his blade around with all of his might. Rhychard parried with the Guardian Sword and countered with the short sword. The elf blocked, and then thrust under Rhychard's arm. The Warrior jumped back, knocking the elf's blade away with the Guardian Sword. The elf kept on the attack, swinging back and forth as he yelled. Rhychard stayed on the defense, blocking with his blades as he kept backing up. All he could do was keep knocking the other's sword to the side, stopping it from skewering him.

Suddenly, Rhychard felt himself backed against the concrete wall between the ramp and parking spaces. Stuck. The elf snarled as he swung his blade toward Rhychard's head. The Warrior didn't block. He just dropped straight to the ground, swinging the Guardian Sword, the voices of Warriors past growling in his ears. The blade sliced through the elf's legs, just below the knees. His agonizing scream filled the parking garage as he fell to the ground. Rhychard drove the iron sword into the creature's chest until he felt the tip hit the concrete floor. The elf grunted, his eyes full of hate, just before he exploded into ashes. "Warrior nine, elf dead."

Twenty-One

"He's dead?" Buttercup just stared at him with her mouth open and her eyes revealing her disbelief. He wasn't sure if it was shock at the news or her still being half asleep. Kree had felt the strain in Rhychard's mind before he pulled into Whispering Oaks about half past four that morning and everyone inside the condo had known what happened by the time he passed through the front door.

"He's dead. So is his partner, two dark elves and a score of gargoyles. They definitely didn't want me to go to church tonight." He tossed his jacket and the harness of swords on the small dining room table and dropped into his recliner. He was exhausted and the main battle hadn't even happened yet. It was going to be a long day.

Buttercup just stared into the air. Surely, a girl of the streets had seen death before, but how up close and personal, Rhychard wasn't sure. "Does this mean I'm safe?"

Rhychard shook his head. "Not until after tonight, and then probably only if we somehow win." He didn't voice how slim he thought their chances were of success. He almost died that night. Vargas was sure to have more of his Void buddies in attendance. It was the timing of everything that was going to be the key. The ritual had to start, but never finish. How was he to empty out a church in just a few minutes?

He needed a nap.

And he had taken one, but only a short one. Dusk blanketed Harbor City as Rhychard stood outside of Harvest Fellowship staring at the shadows that surrounded the giant church. In the dark it appeared as any other structure—lifeless. The tall halogen lamps that towered throughout the parking lot created small circles of light on the asphalt, but even they seemed like gray shadows. Security lights glowed from inside the giant foyer, a giant chandelier of crystal hanging prominently behind the tall tinted glass front. No crosses. Not even on the tall pristine steeple that pointed challengingly at the Heavens. Everything on the outside looked perfect. The grass was crisply manicured. The hedges and palms groomed with precise care. No litter, no cigarette butts, no oil staining the parking spaces. Immaculate.

It was the inside that reeked. For the first time, he noticed the disturbing blanket of wrongness that draped over the property. When you neared the city dump you can smell the garbage from hundreds of yards away. It was the same in feeling the presence of the Void; at least, it was with people steeped in the Way. Harvest Fellowship was a cesspool of evil and it was Adrian's fault. For years the pastor had compromised, watered down Truth to hide the greed and lust for power that really motivated him. That compromise was going to get him killed.

"This really burns my flapjacks," Rhychard spoke into the dawn.

:Righteousness sometimes leads to decisions that are nauseous.: Kree walked along the shore of the streambed behind the church. *:Adrian is repulsive, but the Void more so. Vargas must be stopped.:*

A Gateway would unleash Hell, literally, into their small city allowing the Void a major stronghold into the region. Rhychard took a deep, fortifying breath. Well, no time like the present. "I hope the roof doesn't cave in on me," Rhychard said as he sneaked around the back of the main building and jimmied a window open in the nursery area. He expected an alarm, but there wasn't any loud screeching noise going off. *:Someone's already here.:*

:Pastor Adrian's car is in the garage,: Kree spoke. *:Rhychard, Renny's car is here, as well.:*

Kree's words brought Rhychard to a quick halt. She had promised him to avoid the church and Adrian tonight. What could have been so important as to break that promise. *:Kree…:*

:Tryna is already searching, Warrior. The ellyll will find her. You must focus on the path ahead if we are to stop Vargas.:

Rhychard listened at the nursery door, but heard nothing. He knew the coshey was right, but he had already sacrificed enough for what was right. He couldn't sacrifice any more. He couldn't lose Renny now that he had a chance of getting her back in his life. He wouldn't. His heart wanted him to find Renny, but his mind told him that Kree was right. The best way to protect Renny was to put an end to the ritual that would open the Gateway. He had to wait for Vargas to appear. *Time to find a hiding spot.*

The one thing about church services is that they are all basically the same. Attend one for a month and you have that particular church's pattern down. While other churches may vary slightly, most were almost identical in their programs. The message changes as do the songs, but really, it follows the same blueprint week after week, year after year. Rituals were predictable, even those of setting up for the service to come. Therefore, Rhychard knew just when to sneak into the second floor sound booth and hide, waiting for Vargas to appear. The sound booth was really a small open room facing the auditorium where the sound and lighting crews, as well as the video team, worked their technical magic. Modern day church had turned into a big production.

He could see Joe and Ryan spinning dials and switching cords as the sound of people filing into the sanctuary filtered up to him from the bottom floor. He stood behind a shelf of speaker cables and broken microphones as the smell of sulfur began to permeate the place. He glanced at the two sound men, but they showed no sign of noticing. He shook his head. *How have so many fallen so far?*

:Warrior, Tryna has spotted gargoyles around the steeple and the roof of the parking garage. They seem to be searching for a way inside. There is no sign of your former life mate.:

Where could Renny have been hiding? Or did Adrian have her holed up somewhere? Maybe she left. He gave his head a mental shake. As much as he wanted to, he could not think of that right now. *:Let the games begin then, I guess,:* Rhychard replied.

:I'd much prefer backgammon.:

:Only because you win,:

:Let us hope we win this one.:

Rhychard silently agreed as the praise band began to kick the service into gear. Most of the songs sounded the same to him, so he was able to ignore the music and focus on everything else that was going on. He could sense the energy mix of the Way and the Void around him, knew that Harvest Fellowship wasn't completely lost. There were good people in the congregation, people committed to the righteous path they had chosen. However, it had not been enough to keep the Unseelie from gaining a foothold and eventually a stronghold. It was too late to save the land. Hopefully, he could still save the people.

Pastor Adrian left his seat in the front row, climbed the three blue carpeted steps to the platform and clapped his hands with the music. Minister of Music, James Henderson, brought the song to a close and dutifully stepped back, his small hands resting on the topside of his acoustic guitar. He was giving Adrian a peculiar look, but Rhychard couldn't see a reason for it. Perhaps James was one of the pastor's victims. Maybe he just realized the man was a jerk.

Adrian held up his hands. "Welcome, friends and guests! We are glad you have joined us for this great experience as we begin a new venture here at Harvest Fellowship. You have given up your Saturday night to share in an experience that you will never have again. You have shown that being in church is more important than being in a night club getting drunk. I'm proud of you! And I promise, tonight, you will be justly rewarded for your efforts."

The congregation cheered and clapped. It was more like a pep rally than a church service and Adrian was working the crowd instead of ministering to the people. It had actually surprised Rhychard when Adrian called the congregation to prayer and everyone bowed their heads in solemn silence.

Rhychard needed a look at the sanctuary below and the prayer was a great cover. He just had to get past the two soundmen. He slid a small dagger from his waist and with catlike stealth eased over to where Joe Rubin stood bent over a sound board, focused intently on the sliders he was adjusting. Silencing him wasn't going to be a problem. Keeping Ryan from yelling out, however, was. A foot away from Joe, Rhychard swung and with the handle of his blade struck the young man upside the head in a way that dropped him unconscious to the floor.

Ryan heard the attack and spun in his seat. Rhychard swung backwards, the dagger's pommel catching the older man across the temple, dropping him to the floor. Rhychard jerked his attention to the stage where the band and choir were, worried he had been seen, but everyone's head was still bowed and their eyes closed.

Rhychard surveyed the people below him. He knew most of them, had worshipped with them back before Renny dumped him. Those people had been his friends at one point, but that was before being a Warrior of the Way had consumed him. However, it wasn't the people before him that had changed, not really; it was him. The type of corruption it took to transform Sacred Ground didn't happen overnight. It took years of compromising the little things and ignoring the big things to weaken the power of the Way. They stopped seeing everything as black and white. Rhychard, however, could no longer view things with shades of gray, not since he had been chosen by the Way to be one of its sword bearers. He had seen too much since then to stomach the hypocrisy.

"That dog can't come in here." The voice trembled as it squeaked.

Rhychard peered over the edge and saw the Head Usher backing away from the massive coshey who was escorting Tryna and Buttercup into the sanctuary. *:Tired of waiting?:*

Kree turned his head to peer up at Rhychard. *:Tryna believed a strong visual would assist in getting the people to vacate the church when it was time.:*

Rhychard nodded. *:Expose the corrupt shepherd and shake things up.:* He climbed onto the sound board and then the ledge overlooking the congregation. As he did, he spotted two gargoyles, their leathery hide a dark sheen in the upper corners of the stage. *:The gargoyles have made their way inside. Vargas is making his move.:*

"Hey! How did you get up there?" The Head Usher screamed as he pointed at Rhychard, his head jerked back and forth between Rhychard on the ledge and the trio of misfits walking down the center aisle. He didn't know which broken rule to deal with first and Miles Evans was all about the rules. Rhychard could see the veins on the man's neck throbbing. "You can't be up there."

By then Adrian ceased his praying and the congregation jerked around in their seats to see what the commotion was about. The pastor just stared at all of them. He wasn't surprised to see them there. His face actually held a smirk. He knew what the end game was and could care less if his dirty deeds were about to be exposed. Not everyone was so nonchalant about what Buttercup's presence meant. Looking around, the Warrior noticed several men, as well as a couple of ladies, fidgeting in their seats. *Buttercup's been a busy girl.*

:Gargoyles in every corner and over the doors,: he sent to Kree. *:Watch your backs.:*

The elven hound below sneezed as he shook his head. *:Their stench tickles my nose.:*

Rhychard would have laughed at any other time. Instead, he turned his attention to the man at the pulpit. The Warrior stood, hands on his hips, smiling. "Miles invited me to your new service, and I invited a few of my friends, so here we are." With a wave of his hand, he gestured to the creatures huddled against the ceiling, claws digging into the drywall. "I see you invited your new friends, as well." Rhychard stared at the man at the pulpit, no longer smiling.

People glanced up for the first time and started screaming. In a mass, they began to push toward the center aisle to escape whatever was clawing the walls above them. Rhychard searched the panicked congregation for

Renny, but the woman was nowhere to be seen. It didn't make sense. Her car had been here, so she had to be here. So, why wasn't she in the terrified throng below?

Rhychard glared at Adrian. *What have you done to...* Then Renny's absence wasn't the only thing not adding up.

"I'm here to tell these people what you made me do!" Buttercup was shouting trying to be heard over the commotion of people who had just found out that the Boogeyman was real. It was a good plan and would have worked if Rhychard hadn't jumped the gun and pointed out the gargoyles above them

David Morsetti stood, his arms around his wife, trying to get to an exit. Others Rhychard knew were cowering behind chairs, hoping to hide or at least not be trampled.

Rhychard kept his eyes on Adrian, however, doing his best not to lose focus. Something was off. And then it clicked. Adrian's clothes didn't fit. Pastor Adrian Michaels was too pompous not to be impeccably groomed at all times. Double-breasted suits. Spit-polished shoes. Immaculate hair. Nothing was ever out of place. Now everything was too small, even his hair. His body had a gray pallor and Rhychard knew why James had been staring at Adrian with disgust. Adrian was not Adrian. "Body possession."

The demon was staring directly at him, a smirk stretched across his face. Vargas. Did that mean Adrian was dead? Rhychard had no clue how body possession worked. He really needed Tryna to strengthen his education. He felt a tightening of his chest. If Adrian was now Vargas, where was Renny?

Buttercup couldn't tell that Adrian was no longer the pompous pastor. She stood beside Kree, shouting the obscenities the man had made her do in his quest for power. No one else noticed that the creature before them was not their beloved leader, either. They were too busy trying to get as far away from the creatures crawling the ceiling as possible. More kept showing up, perched over exits, their claws striking out at the nearest victim. *You got off way too easy, Adrian.*

The pastor's eyes were flaming red slits as they narrowed their focus onto the honey-colored lady before him. Rhychard watched as he stretched his arms, the claws of Vargas ripping through human flesh, blood dripping from the open wounds. "You!" He pointed an arm—half demon, half human—at Buttercup. "You should have stayed hidden."

Rhychard reached over his shoulder and drew his sword. The blade glowed a deep blue, its heat filling his hand as the voices of a dozen

Warriors screamed for release. They wanted to slay the demon. Rhychard was okay with that. *:Adrian is Vargas! He's going after Buttercup.:* Rhychard did a springboard leap off the ledge and out over the congregation. Kree roared, sending most of the hysterical mob around them scrambling. Rhychard tucked his head under, did a somersault in the air and landed in a crouch in front of Tryna and her charge. Vargas struck James Henderson across the throat slicing halfway through the man's neck as he gripped a microphone stand and hurled it at Buttercup like a javelin. First blood. The ritual had begun. The Warrior brought his sword up, knocking the metal rod into a too slow gargoyle, sending the creature back against the wall, the stand piercing its chest

"Feed!" Vargas bellowed, his arms outstretched to the dark creatures. "Let their blood be used for our brethren."

"Nooooo!"

Rhychard spun and saw Miles in the talons of one of the gargoyles being carried back up to the ceiling. Before the Warrior could pull his dagger, the creature of the Void bit into the man's neck ripping out his Adam's apple. The man's blood dripped onto the people below. Panic. Screams echoed off the walls. Some tried to push through the exits only to be torn apart.

:Kree, clear a path and get these people out of here.: Rhychard leaped onto the back of a chair while shoving some balding man to the ground. *:I'm going after Vargas!:* He ran across the back of the chairs, leaping over the heads of people as he made his way to the front. One couple he recognized was down on their knees, hands clasped tight, praying with loud voices. Rhychard found David and Sylvia, both searching for a way out. The Warrior grabbed David's shoulder and pointed toward Kree. "Follow the giant dog! He's here to help." He then continued after the demon.

Vargas brought the ceiling down around two doors blocking those exits. One of the leathery beasts swooped down on Rhychard, claws reaching. The Warrior dropped down between two rows as he swung his blue blade, severing the creature's arms. Back on his feet, he sheathed his sword as he reached into his jacket for his knives. With precision throws he flung one after the other at the gargoyles over the east door. They screamed as they burst into a shower of ash. Rhychard grabbed the praying couple yanking them to their feet and shoved them to the door. "Pray and run! Get people out of here and across the street. Now!"

With his knives gone, Rhychard yanked his sword out of its sheath with his right hand while scooping up a hymnal with the other. He flung the book at Adrian/Vargas, striking the demon on the shoulder. It was enough to distract the beast and bring his attention back to Rhychard.

Vargas screamed and with a sudden push ripped through the rest of Adrian's body. Blood and body parts covered the cowering congregation. Miss Wilson passed out and dropped to the floor. The demon's eyes glowed red as he focused on Rhychard. "Come to die, Warrior?"

They always have to talk. Why can't they just fight? Rhychard strengthened his grip on the sword with both hands, the point aimed at Vargas. He said nothing as he approached.

Vargas turned, his birdlike feet planted, ready to fight. Rhychard approached with slow, determined steps. There was no way he was getting out of here alive, if demons were ever really alive.

Then the creature thrust his arm out and a red bolt of demonic power shot for Rhychard's head, followed by another and another. With the blue sword Rhychard deflected each one, doing his best to send it into some piece of furniture or portion of wall. The Warrior kept edging closer.

Then Vargas lunged and Rhychard fell backwards rolling to his left, sword swinging around as he leaped back up to his feet. Vargas swung with his arm, his claws raking Rhychard's left shoulder before he could bring the sword back around. It was like fire burning into him as he screamed. White dots of agony exploded in front of him as he swung the Guardian Sword around, trying to back the demon up.

The creature just laughed as he toyed with the Warrior. "You've failed. Warrior! You can't stop me." His laughter was like a dog growling. "The Gateway will open. Nothing can stop it."

:Warrior, the place is empty of all who can move,: Kree mind spoke to him. *:It is enough.:*

:Renny…:

:Tryna is searching.:

Rhychard staggered, his left arm useless due to the demon. He braced himself for another attack. He had to give Tryna time to find Renny. He stood as straight as he could as he faced the demon. With the tip of his sword, he waved the creature on. "Let the game begin."

Vargas stood and laughed. "Killing you will be as much fun as it was killing the pastor's little toy. Poor girl never knew what she was being groomed for until it was too late. And now you will…Aaaarrrgghh!!!" The demon roared as he clutched at a golden pole that suddenly thrust through his heart and chest. The creature's scream was deafening as his head jerked back, his claws reaching for the girl behind him. Rhychard jumped in the air, swinging the Guardian Sword with both hands. The blade flared hot. The voices howled as the sword sliced through the demon's neck, severing his head from his shoulder. Suddenly, the demon exploded with black flames and was gone.

When Rhychard uncovered his eyes all he saw was Buttercup standing there with the golden pole holding the American flag. Tears streamed down her face as she stared at the sulfurous smoke floating in the air that once was Vargas. The Warrior approached her, wrapping her into his jacket with his damaged arm. She fell into him, the sobs erupting from her frail body.

Rhychard held his sword in front of him, waiting for the few gargoyles that remained to attack. However, with their leader gone they just spun in the air and flew off leaving the place littered with carcasses and broken building.

The church was shaking as chunks of ceiling began to fall around them. The magic that had begun to open the way to the Nether now had nowhere to go and was building in on itself.

"C'mon, lady. Time to go."

:Warrior, quick. Tryna found Renny in the pastor's office.:

Rhychard led Buttercup through the chaos and wreckage around them until he reached the office of Adrian Michaels. Shelves were knocked over, books strewn across the floor, windows shattered. It was like a tornado had happened within the small office. The only place untouched was the cherry wood desk in the middle of the room.

Renny lay on top of the desk, Kree's chin draped over her torso. Blood pooled under her, her body ripped open. Rhychard felt his knees buckle under him and it was Buttercup that held him up this time. "Is she…?"

Tryna looked up into his eyes, tears trickled down her cheeks. "She is beyond Kree's gift. He can only prolong the inevitable for a short while. The damage is too extensive. I'm sorry, Rhychard. I'm truly sorry."

He staggered to where Renny lay. He brushed the blond hair out of her closed eyes as tears streamed down his face. He wanted to scream, but the hand of emotions that clutched at his heart stole his breath, as well. He leaned down and kissed her cold lips, his tears falling onto her face. "I'm so sorry."

Her eyes flickered open and she gripped his hand with hers. "No," she said, her voice a distant whisper. "I'm the one who is sorry. I gave up on you. On us."

Buttercup moved to stand by the ellyll, tears in her own eyes as she rubbed at her arms.

Rhychard laid a hand on Renny's forehead. "You weren't supposed to be here."

The dying woman coughed, blood trickling out of her mouth and down her cheek. "I wanted to help you. I owed it to you. I wanted to confront Adrian." Her body heaved as another coughing fit wracked her body, knocking Kree's chin from her chest. His silver fur dripped with her blood.

Rhychard leaned down and kissed her, his tears mixing with hers. "I love you," he whispered as he pulled away, but Renny Saunders was already gone. He gripped her body to him as he cried out his anguish. She wasn't supposed to be there. They were going to make it!

:The building is about to go. We need to leave.: Kree nudged the Warrior with his damp nose.

Buttercup reached out and pulled at the Warrior's arm as more of the ceiling caved in. "Please. We must get out of here," she said.

Tryna touched his arm. "Save the living."

He nodded as he stood, finally sheathing the Guardian Sword. He gripped Buttercup's hand and headed for the pastor's door. "Let's go."

Tryna rode atop Kree as the giant elven hound followed Buttercup. Rhychard held her hand as he led her out of the building and across the parking lot. The parking garage was a pile of rubble as car alarms blared. It almost appeared like an earthquake had hit the church property. Emergency sirens sounded and Rhychard knew that soon the place would be swarming with police officers and fire and rescue personnel. He wanted to be long gone, but at the edge of the woods he stopped and watched as Harvest Fellowship imploded on itself, the demon ritual failing without its sacrifice.

Rhychard took a deep breath, the image of Renny's mutilated torso fixed forever in his mind. "Why did Vargas kill her before the ritual? Wasn't she first blood?"

Tryna's eyes stared at the collapsing building. "No. She was the sacrifice that enabled his possession of Mr. Michaels' body. Most everything evil does requires a sacrifice. As Kendalais said, 'Life is in the blood, therefore, the power and energy of life resides in the blood.' I'm afraid that was to be her purpose all along."

Rhychard just stood there and stared. *Goodbye, Renny.* A lone tear muddied his dirty cheek. *I'm sorry.*

Buttercup pulled his arm, trying to take his attention off the broken church. The Warrior nodded as he turned and led the odd band of heroes deeper into the woods away from the carnage that had once been Harvest Fellowship. "Let's go home. I need a nap."

About the Author

Robbie Cox lives in sunny Florida where he spends his days taxiing the family to various places while jotting down the many crazy thoughts inside his head. He enjoys a freelance career where he writes for several magazines sharing some of his interesting viewpoints on life and those around him. He can usually be found on his back porch surrounded by family while he enjoys a cigar, a scotch, and the many characters that talk to him inside his head.

Connect with Robbie online:

Facebook - https://www.facebook.com/robbiecoxauthor

Twitter - http://twitter.com/CoxRobbie

Website - http://www.robbiecox.net/

Made in the USA
Columbia, SC
20 November 2017